# ARE WE THE MASTERS OF OUR OWN MINDS ?



*Or are there other powers on Earth stronger than we, capable of controlling our thoughts and actions by long-distance suggestion?*

*THE TRANSCENDENT MAN is a novel about a very possible future ruled by a dictatorship more effective than any before—*

*BECAUSE THE DICTATORS' ONLY WEAPON IS INVISIBLE—AN ENORMOUS AND IRREVOCABLE POWER OVER MEN'S MINDS.*

Books by Jerry Sohl

THE HAPLOIDS

COSTIGAN'S NEEDLE

THE ALTERED EGO

POINT ULTIMATE

PRELUDE TO PERIL

Published by Bantam Books

# THE TRANSCENDENT MAN

BY JERRY SOHL

Bantam Books

New York

THE TRANSCENDENT MAN

*A Bantam Book / published by arrangement with Rinehart & Company, Inc.*

PRINTING HISTORY

*Rinehart edition published April 1953*
*Bantam edition published August 1959*

*Grateful acknowledgment is made to Longmans, Green & Company, Inc., for permission to reprint an excerpt from their* PRAGMATISM, *copyright 1907 by William James, copyright renewed 1934.*



---

*Bantam Books are published by Bantam Books, Inc. Its trade-mark, consisting of the words "Bantam Books" and the portrayal of a bantam, is registered in the U. S. Patent Office and in other countries. Marca Registrada. Printed in the United States of America. Bantam Books, Inc., 25 W. 45th St., New York 36, N. Y.*

---

FOR MY MOTHER

*I firmly disbelieve, myself, that our human experience is the highest form of experience extant in the universe. I believe rather that we stand in much the same relation to the whole of the universe as our canine and feline pets do to the whole of human life. They inhabit our drawing rooms and libraries. They take part in scenes of whose significance they have no inkling. They are merely tangent to curves of history the beginnings and ends and forms of which pass wholly beyond their ken. So we are tangent to the wider life of things.*

*William James*

# 1

Martin Enders saw a strange thing. He *felt* it first—even before he heard the laughter.

It happened after he had given his credentials to the soldier at the gate. The corporal puzzled over them for a moment, then conducted him inside the gatehouse, where he presented him to the officer in charge, an ascetic-looking youngster who carried an air of not trusting even his own senses.

The lieutenant compared the picture on the card with the man standing before him. He continued to stare at Martin as if he would like to memorize the position of every pore, every hair in the eyebrows.

"Do I look like someone you know?" Martin asked, irked by the intense examination.

"No, why?"

"I thought you were trying to place me."

"You will find it the rule here at Park Hill. Everyone and everything is double-checked and cross-checked. I make a point of never forgetting a face. Where did you get this card?"

"From the attorney general's office."

"Whom did you expect to see?"

Martin gave him the letter he had ready in his hand. "Dr. Eric Penn, Lieutenant. I'm from *National Scene.*"

The officer scowled, took the letter. "Nobody can see Dr. Penn," he said as he unfolded it. His eyebrows jumped upward as he saw the letterhead. He glanced at Martin, then went back to the letter. A lip mover, the lieutenant formed each word as he read. When he finished, he handed it back, opened the counter gate and ushered Martin to a chair beside his desk.

"You understand the precautions," the lieutenant said.

"Security, I suppose."

The officer nodded. His manner had changed, but there was still an edge of suspicion in his glance, the way he held his lips, the things he did with his hands.

"I have to ask a lot of questions," he said. "There are several forms. You will have to be fingerprinted."

"Is that all necessary?"

"I'm afraid so—even with that letter from the commanding general."

Martin grumblingly submitted. He was measured, weighed, his signature compared, his fingerprints matched with those on the card. His voice was recorded on a small tape. It was only after Martin stepped through a steel-rimmed doorway that the lieutenant's tension lessened. No bells had rung; no lights had flashed. The lieutenant actually managed a faint smile as he returned Martin's wrist watch, metal belt buckle and coins. He was even helpful, pointing out the administration building at the end of a long walk several blocks distant.

It was while Martin was on the long sidewalk from the guard station at the gate to the administration building that the incident occurred.

The avenue was bush-lined and as straight as a ruler. As Martin walked down it, he had a feeling the lieutenant at the gate was watching him. He wondered if anyone in the building up ahead was aware of his approach. Forrest Killian must have moved down the same sidewalk three months before; there was no way of telling if Forrest had felt the same way.

At a point on the walk halfway between the gatehouse and the administration building Martin experienced the first odd sensation—a feeling that a cold wind was blowing through him, varying in strength, chilling his blood, clouding his mind, then lifting capriciously.

Then he heard laughter. It came from not more than twenty feet to his right. He turned his head to see who it was and stopped so that he could look through a narrow space between the bushes.

A child was playing there in the October sun, a chubby, dark-haired boy Martin guessed to be about seven years of age. The blue-eyed lad stood on the neat grass watching a transparent, red-hued sphere floating in the air. He was talking to it. The globe hung motionless, then dipped and rose as if at command and each time it did, the child giggled. Suddenly the globe came to a quick stop; then it whirled about crazily and—vanished. Peals of childish laughter followed.

Martin was about to turn away from this wonder and collect himself when new cold waves of faintly tingling feeling swept over him, making his flesh crawl. The boy had stiffened, his eyes were closed and he concentrated; his little lips were pressed thin and his forehead was furrowed with effort.

In an area just in front of the boy and a little higher than his head there was a disturbance. Then a black thing materialized and plopped to the ground, only to skitter away. It was a cat. The lad's laughter followed it into the bushes near Martin.

The youngster saw Martin and instantly the laughter died and the bright, piercing eyes glazed. For an instant the child stood there. Then he ran away across the grass, his little legs pumping furiously.

# 2

"I agreed to a life story only because I thought it might do biology some good and that it might encourage some youngster," Dr. Penn said. "Now you tell me you're going to literally *live* with me, Mr. Enders."

Martin smiled. "I'll wager you didn't learn all you know about biology just through a casual interview, Dr. Penn. You've had to live with it."

Dr. Penn laughed. "I trust you won't have to live with me as long as I've had to live with biology. I'm sure you'll find me much simpler than biology. But frankly"—he looked at Martin with quickening severity—"I don't see how I can spare the time."

"I'm sure you won't even notice me when you're busy, Dr. Penn. I'll just accumulate my questions for a period when you're not working."

"Those periods, you'll find, are few and far between."

"I'll chance it," Martin said. "I take it you read *National Scene?"*

"I'm a subscriber. I've taken it for years. You people do a very thorough job." The doctor ran a hand over a rack of corncob pipes, selected one and filled it from a humidor. "This is one of my 'Missouri meerschaum' pipes," he said. "I get all kinds for Christmas, but there's something about a corncob that I like. That's the sort of thing you use in your character sketches, isn't it?"

Martin nodded. "Personal habits are a relatively minor point, Doctor. You see, *National Scene* endeavors to get inside a man. We try to tell how he thinks, why he thinks that way, how he came to be where he is, why he is considered important."

"Who says I'm important?" Dr. Penn looked over the top of the flame of the kitchen match he was using to light his pipe. He was an enormous man with a hawklike nose; the match was held in long, thin fingers. His black eyebrows were bushy and gave his eyes a hypnotic quality.

"The Nobel Prize, Doctor. The long list of accomplishments you have after your name in *American Men of Science."*

There was something odd about this man. For as long as he could remember, Martin had been able to feel things about people. It was something more than intuition, this ability to sense another's emotions; when he had first discovered that the talent was not widespread, he ceased advertising the fact that he possessed it, but, silently thankful of its presence, had used it constantly.

When a person's fear, pride, ambition or anger fairly shouted its existence to him, he had often been amazed to find that others in the same room were unaware of it. He considered it a natural attribute, much as some people are gifted with perfect pitch.

What puzzled him about Dr. Penn was that the man exuded none of the usual things. There was a latent force there, Martin felt certain. But just what it was he could only guess. His only conclusion could be that the usual things were not going to work at all with this man.

Dr. Penn blew out the match. "You see this office?" A sweep of his arm covered the entire room. "What do you see here? Does it look as if I work here? A desk. Chairs. Lamps. A typewriter. A telephone. Do you see a test tube or a microscope? I only came here because this is where I come when I have an appointment. I can't see anyone from the outside in my other office. What does that do to your story, Mr. Enders?"

"It means we move to your other office," he said.

The doctor sucked on his pipe and shook his head. Smoke eddied about his short-cut grey hair and the faded blue eyes beneath the heavy eyebrows were almost obscured by it. The man still conveyed nothing to Martin.

"It means I will be able to see you only a short time each day," the doctor said. "No one except 'authorized personnel,' as the army puts it, can go into the laboratory. Is it worth it to you and your magazine to confine your interview to the few minutes a day I will be able to see you here?"

"I've been assigned to the story," Martin said doggedly. Then he smiled. "You will find *National Scene* very thorough, Doctor." He reached into his inner coat pocket, produced an envelope and drew out two letters. "These will verify that I have passed my loyalty test and that I have been approved for classified material." He passed them over. The doctor drew glasses from his breast pocket and read the letters of authority.

"You and your magazine are more than merely very thorough," he said. "You people are damned thorough. With this"—he strummed the letters with the open fingers of his right hand—"there is no way for me to stand in your way, Mr. Enders. How long do you intend to stay? And where? Have you thought of that? Of course you haven't."

Dr. Penn picked up a telephone directory. "There is probably a vacancy at the permanent barracks. Avon Ridge is too far away for commuting. Besides, Colonel Sherrington would not allow you to do that." He riffled through the pages, found a number, called it and made the arrangements.

"You will be in Building P-4," he said to Martin, making a note of it on a pad. "I'll point it out to you when we leave."

"Thanks. I hope I'm not causing you too much trouble."

"You are. But what's on your mind?"

"There are a few preliminary questions I'd like to ask you now, if you don't mind. The answers may help me ask questions of a more specific nature later on."

The doctor looked at his wrist watch. "It's ten past three. Suppose I give you half an hour. I told them at the laboratory I'd be gone only a short time. Frankly, I thought I'd be able to discourage you." He smiled. "Go ahead, Mr. Enders, let's play twenty questions."

Martin took out a notebook. "I hope this note-taking doesn't frighten you, Dr. Penn. If I want to quote you directly, I'll let you know. I can't possibly remember everything."

"Why not?" The doctor chuckled.

"What sort of a project are you working on?"

The doctor slowly withdrew the pipe from his mouth and stared at him in amusement.

"Come now, you don't expect me to tell you that, do you?" He grinned and showed yellowed teeth. "Why do they have such a high fence around this reservation? A mouse can't go in or out without being electrocuted or setting off an alarm."

"Suppose I tell you you're working on regeneration, Dr. Penn? Don't you remember I have access to classified material?"

The doctor nodded. "I had forgotten. Where did you learn that?"

"Just picked it up on my way here. I had to go all the way to Washington for my security permit."

"Of course." The doctor leaned back in his swivel chair, put his hands behind his head and rocked gently. The chair squeaked. "I've never had time to oil this thing," he said, getting up. "It's not conducive to thought that way." He walked to the lone window in the office with an easy, effortless stride for such a big man.

"If you were to look at this research reservation from the air," Dr. Penn said, "you'd see that it is in the form of a hexagon. This administration building stands about halfway between the center and the east gate, the one you came through. In each segment of the hexagon, with the exception of the east one, there is a different research project.

"There are five segment heads, each in charge of his own section. Mine happens to be the one just north of the east gate. I like to think of Penn Project as one that will help and not hinder humanity; it is different from the others here, you see. We in our segment are not trying to blow mankind apart. We're trying to put him back together again. To the military, this is probably a relatively unimportant project. It's a wonder to me it was started at all.

"All of us live in the segment in which we work. The bachelors are housed in a permanent barracks, such as the kind you are to stay in. Each segment has its own cafeteria, exchange, commissary, tavern, movie—that is so that personnel of the various segments will not intermingle. I'm probably boring you."

"You're not boring me, Doctor. Go on."

The doctor moved to the desk, opened the humidor to refill his pipe. "One thing worries me. You've been classified for top secret material, but do you have sense enough not to use it in what you write?"

Martin reddened. "How else can I study you and what you're doing unless I know *what* you're doing? Of course nothing of a secret nature will be revealed."

The doctor lit his pipe again, leaned back reflectively. "If you were a worm I could cut you in two and both parts would grow. But you're not. If I cut you in two, both parts die. Why?

"Our bodies are subject to wear and tear. What if our skin rubbed off, our nails ground down and our hair fell out? So we have some faculty of restoration, you see, but not much. It is confined to healing a cut finger wherein the damaged cells are replaced by new ones. Oh, if a nail is torn off it will grow back. That's a case of accidental regeneration in man. This exceeds mere wound healing. But the loss of a whole limb is irreparable."

"I've heard that some animals grow new tails."

"You've heard correctly, Mr. Enders. The newt does; it can grow a leg or a tail. It's a lower form of life. The higher you go on the scale of animal types, the more curtailed are the regenerative capacities.

"The protozoa, the simplest form, single cells of protoplasm, restore themselves when cut into small pieces, the only condition being there must be a bit of the nucleus in each piece.

"The hydras are able to develop new individuals from cuttings. They belong to the multicellular type. Squids, eye-bearing tentacles of snails, legs of spiders, all the appendages of crustacea and insects and limbs of fish and amphibians—they all grow again after injury."

The doctor shook his head sadly. "Evolution has hurt our power of restoring an arm or leg. Instead, we have a method of continuous repair that works while we live. The nearly total loss of regenerative power has been the price of our evolution."

"But you're working on it."

The doctor smiled. "Yes, we're working on it."

The phone rang.

"Dr. Penn speaking," he said. He tamped tobacco into his pipe with his free hand while he listened. His movements slowed as he became interested in what was said on the phone. Soon they stopped altogether. "You know I gave the order," he said quietly, but his eyes hardened. "You were informed along with the rest; I don't see why it should be such a surprise to you."

Dr. Penn forgot his pipe on the desk, turned his chair around to face away from Martin.

"I realize there are avenues other than the one we are going down, Doctor," Dr. Penn said. "But this one happens to be the one we're on right now." He nodded his head. "As I've told you time and time again, there has to be a leader, Dr. Merrill. Otherwise a project like this would get nowhere. I am that leader. I will take your suggestion and think about it, but until we complete the current tests I don't see how—Oh, now. Look, Doctor . . . Now wait a minute. All right. I'll be right down." He turned and put the phone back in the cradle.

"I'm sorry, Mr. Enders. I've got to go to the lab, but I want you to stay right here until I get back. I shouldn't be gone very long. I have a jeep out front. I don't think I'd better take you with me on this trip." He hurried out of the room.

With Dr. Penn gone, the office lost its life. The doctor's forceful personality had eddied about the room like something alive and now that his deep voice was no longer echoing from the walls, the place seemed deserted.

Martin slumped in his chair, letting his long legs push out on the floor before him. He lit a cigarette and saw that his hand was shaking.

*Steady, old man. But don't forget you're probably in danger. You know what General Deems said. Relax but don't fail to be ready. Somebody—who?—could be watching you.*

He yawned, got up and walked to the window. He was in time to see the doctor pull away from the building in his jeep. As he stood there idly looking out over the area to the east, the sounds of the building came to him: the scraping of a chair on the floor above, the faint clatter of a typewriter, the ringing of a phone in a distant room.

It was all normal. It could have been anywhere on any military reservation in the country. Why should he expect it to be different? Of course there was the boy, the sphere and the cat. . . . *That* made a difference.

He turned his back on the window. Before him was the simple office, just as Dr. Penn had described it. Desk. Pipe rack. Lamp. Typewriter. Chairs. Telephone. What was that other? Two frames and easels. Nobel Prize citations? They looked more like photographs.

Martin walked over behind the desk and caught his breath for two reasons at what he saw there. First, the girl in the one photograph was beautiful. Not because her hair was lovely and yellow or because she was full-lipped and clear-skinned. There were many girls like that. It was her eyes. They were so—ethereal, he decided. They made her look sincere and loving and they gave her face a spirit of animation that attracted him. He decided she must be Dr. Penn's daughter.

The first picture gave him a pleasant glow. The second shocked him, for it was a picture of the child who had played with the sphere and the cat. There was the thick, black hair, the same mischievous blue eyes, the expressive mouth. There could be no doubt; this was the boy. The facial characteristics both pictures had in common suggested they were brother and sister.

He savagely crushed his cigarette in the desk ashtray because of a fleeting feeling that he was being very foolish in thinking anything was wrong. So far there had been no reason to doubt or suspect anything. Dr. Penn seemed all right. The fact that he was a difficult man to read with that special sense of Martin's was no indication he was anything he shouldn't have been. As far as the girl was concerned—well, her picture gave promise of something else. And the kid? He looked like a red-blooded youngster—except for what he had been doing on the lawn.

But the finger was being pointed at Dr. Penn. It was being pointed from a high place. And high places had a habit of looking into things.

I should have never agreed to help General Deems, he told himself. I should have turned him down cold. Let him do his own dirty work, just as I said.

But it had been explained so carefully, so logically . . .

Three days ago he had been sitting with four other men around a limed-oak conference table in the eleventh-floor editorial offices of *National Scene* magazine in Chicago. It was a rainy day and occasionally a puff of wind from Lake Michigan a half mile away came through one of the partly open windows to clear the air of cigarette and cigar smoke and to rustle a few of the many papers before the men at the table.

"This is everything we've got," Lovett Wilson, a managing editor, said, rolling a cigar around in his mouth and indicating the array of papers. "It's hardly a start."

"These pix are old," Caldwell Chonkey said, as if that relegated the project to insignificance. "I don't get it." Chonkey was the magazine's Chicago picture man. His was the battle to provide more pictures per page, but it was a losing battle. *National Scene* was not a picture magazine.

"What are you talking about?" Jimmy Simpson, the chief editorial research man dug through a stack of papers, pulled out a picture.

"Don't tell me where we got that," Chonkey said, refusing to look at it. "It was probably taken at his high-school graduation."

"You're wrong. It's the Nobel Prize acceptance photo."

"Shaking hands and all that. Photographic cliché. Every magazine, syndicate and weekly newspaper has had a crack at that one. You might as well throw it away."

Denton Myers tapped his teeth with the sharpened end of a pencil and shook his head. "We'll just have to own up that Dr. Eric Penn isn't picture-minded. What about AP? UP? NEA? Chonkey, have you tried the *Trib?* The *Sun-Times?*"

"And the *News?*" Chonkey looked terribly pained. "Ever since I got wind of this I've been out after pictures. If Penn was a politico we'd have a bushel of prints. These scientists are just camera-shy. Nobody's got a new picture, Mr. Myers. Believe me."

"I suppose. I suppose."

Chonkey squirmed. This was in his department and it irked him that Dr. Penn never had had the foresight to have some pictures taken.

"What about his two kids?" It was Wilson and he was looking at Chonkey. The picture man slumped lower in his chair.

"Don't blame me because they're not a picture family. Maybe Dr. Penn isn't as big as we think he is."

Jimmy Simpson held up a paper. "Virginia Penn. She's twenty-three. Robert is just a kid. First or second grade."

"But surely a family would have a photograph," Myers insisted.

Chonkey looked at Martin for help.

"We're not a picture magazine," Martin said. "Let's quit riding Chonkey. I'm sure he'd have something if it were available. We can use what we have, if necessary."

"Thanks," Chonkey said with relief.

"Hell, we're not riding Chonkey."

"Sorry, Chonkey."

"I'll get a picture when I get down there," Martin said. "He must have some around somewhere."

"The thing may not pan out, anyway," Wilson said. "In that case we won't need one."

"Don't say that, Willie," Martin said. "You're making it sound uninteresting."

"Well, we don't have much to go on. The fact that he okayed the story surprised the New York office."

Denton Myers picked up the sheaf of papers before him, thumbed through them. "I wonder why he was ever chosen. If it weren't for his scientific achievements, he'd be nothing at all. This hullabaloo about scientists! Personally, I prefer a big promoter, a man who can influence hundreds of people through his personality. Scientists are such cold potatoes."

"Maybe you're just lost in the realm of pure thought," Wilson said. "It takes a certain aptitude."

"All right. But you know what I mean. He was born in Wisconsin, it says here. Went to Pointer College, took his master's at Windsor, got his doctorate at New Howard. Dull, isn't it? Taught for years at Billingsley and performed the research there that netted him the Nobel Prize while he was there."

"We know all that, Denny," Wilson said. "Tell us something we don't know."

"That's where I come in."

Wilson turned to Martin. "Well . . ."

"I don't have anything yet," Martin said. "But the way I get it, Dr. Penn's been helpful in national defense for many years. He's offered some ideas the military has been glad to get. He has the Nobel Prize. He has been elevated, achieving a place in the upper strata of the scientific minds of this country. Now he takes a job with the government at Park Hill, something he wouldn't do during the war. Right?"

"Last September, to be exact," Simpson said. "I've got the date right here." He shuffled through several sheets.

"You mean more than a year ago, not last month."

"Yeah."

"Incidentally," Wilson said, "we've wired Washington for permission to get on the reservation. Park Hill is a tough nut to crack."

"How about Dr. Penn?"

"Martin will do all right," Myers said. "He's been kicked out of better places, haven't you?"

"Don't rub it in."

"Is everything set, then?" Lovett Wilson looked around at the group. "Any questions?"

"A month ago New York sent a wire to Dr. Penn," Myers said. "He wired back a week ago accepting. What more do we need?"

"I'd rather work from scratch anyway," Martin said.

"It ought to be a good piece," Wilson said. "Different. It's got unique angles, the reservation, the research project, all that."

"Remember the picture, Martin," Chonkey said. "If you don't get one in right away for the artist, it won't be a cover story."

"Want me to take one of your cameras with me?"

"I can see you carrying a camera into Park Hill," Simpson said.

"I never thought of that."

The chime clock on Lovett Wilson's office wall struck five times. When the last tone sounded, there was a general movement of chairs away from the table.

"Take as long as you like on this one," Wilson said, coming over and extending a beefy hand. "You seem to work better when you can take your time."

Martin took the hand.

"Better bone up on biology before you go," Simpson said, his hand on Martin's shoulder. "We've got a whole slew of stuff in the library."

"No, thanks," Martin said. "I'll take it from first grade on up as Dr. Penn gives it."

"Good luck," Myers called, going out.

When they were gone, Martin gathered up a few of the papers he wanted, put them in his brief case. Lovett Wilson stood by, idly watching him. When Martin was ready to go, Wilson helped him on with his coat.

"There's one thing more," the managing editor said.

"What's that?"

"I could show you the correspondence, but I won't. I'll tell you instead. There's pressure on this thing."

"Pressure? What kind of pressure?"

"From New York. From the top."

"D'Orsey himself, eh? Got any idea why?"

Wilson shook his head. "I didn't want to mention it before the rest of them."

"I had wondered about the man."

"You mean Penn, of course."

"Yes. There isn't much there."

"Not much that meets the eye, perhaps. There must be something underneath we don't know about."

"At least that ought to make it more interesting."

"One other thing."

Martin waited to hear what it was.

"New York wanted to know who we'd assigned to it. Three days ago they wanted your picture."

"I'll be damned!"

"Don't ask me. It's just peculiar."

"This never happened before. Maybe I'm up for a raise."

"You'd better get going, funny boy."

When the elevator doors opened on the main floor, Associate Editor Martin Enders's mind was already pounding away at plans for the story. He'd have to wait for a pass for Park Hill Research Reservation before he started, and if he knew Washington, it would probably be days before it arrived. In the meantime, he could scour the morgues of every newspaper. Perhaps a trip to Dr. Penn's home town, the schools he attended, a few interviews with students he had had would be a good starter. By that time perhaps the pass would have arrived.

Martin moved automatically with the group leaving the elevator cage, walked past the cigarette counter and through the revolving doors to the street.

When the man came up to him Martin at first thought he was someone he knew. The stranger was a clean-cut, neatly dressed man with a bright look about him.

"Martin Enders?" the man asked.

Martin nodded.

The man withdrew a leather folder from an inner pocket. He opened it. There was a picture of him inside. The message beneath it said his name was Kenneth Aldrich and that he was an agent for the Federal Bureau of Investigation.

# 3

"I must ask you to come with me," the agent said.
"Am I under arrest?" Martin asked in surprise.
The FBI man smiled. "No. I'm not arresting you. Is there any reason I should?" The agent seemed amused at Martin's bewilderment.
"At least several," Martin said in recovery. "I just wondered which one. Would you mind explaining?"
The agent was grinning now. "You were up there a long time." He pointed in the direction of the eleventh floor.
"You've been waiting?"
"Hours. Couldn't tap you before it was over. Will you come now?"
"You still haven't explained."
"I'll do that on the way." He looked at his wrist watch. "It's getting late and there's a plane waiting."
Martin grudgingly gave his approval, wondering where this would put him on the cover story he was supposed to do.
The FBI man led him to a car where a man behind the wheel started the motor as they approached. Once inside, Martin was thrown against the rear cushion as the car lurched out into traffic with a squeal of protesting tires and a clashing of gears.
"Is this an emergency?" Martin asked after he caught his breath.
"Frankly, Mr. Enders, I don't know how to answer that question," the agent replied. "I do know I'm supposed to take you to Washington, D. C."
"Why, for heaven's sake?"
The agent's grin returned. "To see a man who wants to meet you."
"Now who would that be?"
"A man named Walter Deems. Name mean anything to you?"
"Never heard of him."
"I'm only guessing when I say he probably knows you pretty well."
"Who is Walter Deems?"

"He happens to be in Intelligence."

The car sped through a gate at the Chicago airport and slowed to a stop on the hangar apron where a small passenger plane was warming up. In a few minutes they were in the air, heading east.

Martin talked more with the FBI man but was unable to learn anything further. The agent did not seem reluctant to discuss the matter; he simply knew no more than he had already told.

They landed at Washington and again there was a car waiting. Once again there was the squealing of tires on the getaway, only Martin was prepared this time. Some minutes later the car slid to a stop in front of a small white stone building.

An armed soldier blocked their way momentarily. Another soldier shined a flashlight beam in their faces and on the agent's identification card. They were allowed to pass into the building.

Martin was conducted to a room at the end of a hall where a large man in army uniform with two stars on his shoulders sat behind a large walnut desk. There was a picture of the President on the wall behind him. The army man, his grey hair bristling beyond his receding hairline, his eyes snapping brightly as he saw Martin, rose and offered a smile and his hand.

"Glad you could come, Mr. Enders." His voice was full and resonant and carried an edge of authority. "I am General Walter Deems."

"I didn't have much choice about coming." Martin heard the door close softly behind him.

"Sit down, sit down," the general said, indicating a chair. "Of course you didn't. Have a cigarette?"

"Thanks." As the general provided a light, Martin said, "Is this cigarette by any chance one for a condemned man?"

General Deems smiled, sat down, studied Martin's face. "Whether you realize it or not, you have just become a very valuable man, Mr. Enders. *National Scene* has helped us solve a bad problem."

"I don't see how."

"You have been assigned to do a cover story on Dr. Eric Penn, haven't you?"

Martin looked at the man in astonishment. "How did you know about that?"

"It is our business to know."

"That explains the pressure, then."

"Pressure?"

"The New York office wanted very badly to have the Penn story started. But why is the army interested? I thought Dr. Penn was working for the army."

"Ever hear of the CIC? The Counter-Intelligence Corps?"

"Of course."

"This is it. You're in the main office right now," Deems said.

"I'm very much impressed. Now, will you tell me what this all has to do with me and the job I'm supposed to do for *National Scene?*"

The general chuckled. "It may have nothing to do with it. That depends on you." He lit his own cigarette. "We need your help. Your *personal* help."

"In what way?"

"We want you to work for us while you are doing the Penn story."

Martin smiled wanly. "Cloak-and-dagger stuff? I'm afraid you've got the wrong man, General. That's not up my alley."

"You have a fine record for your services in World War Two."

"You fellows are pretty thorough, aren't you? Looking up a man's army record! How come I get all this personal attention?"

"We mean to be thorough. You are the logical man for the job, whether you like it or not."

"You haven't been thorough enough. I could have told you you're way off base figuring me for an undercover job."

"You were selected for the Penn story over all the rest on the magazine, Mr. Enders."

"I thought there was something funny about doing a story on Dr. Eric Penn. He's not the usual story material. Nothing really startling, no glamour, nothing earth-shaking. So now it appears the CIC has manufactured the job and has sold *National Scene* a bill of goods for some purpose of its own. I don't mind telling you I don't like the smell of it."

General Deems blew out his cheeks. "You wouldn't be talking like that if you knew why we want you to go to Park Hill."

"I don't want to know, General Deems," Martin said a little more kindly. "First of all, I resent the fact that the military steps into private business to tell it what to do."

"It's an emergency."

"You obviously convinced them that it was. Second, nobody discussed it with me. In the military game I'm suddenly tagged. I'm it. I've got to risk my neck. Third, I don't play that way, General. Fourth, I learned in the army not to volunteer for a damned thing. And last of all, I'm through with anything to do with anything military. Period. I got my belly full of it during the war. I saw man's inhumanity to man and I don't want to see it again."

"You *are* bitter, aren't you?" the general said softly. "Well, I don't blame you. But you have proven initiative. You have a high I. Q. Why don't you let me explain what we want you to do?"

"Why don't you send one of your own men on this job, whatever it is? I might fumble the ball."

General Deems was grave. "We did send one of our men. His name was Forrest Killian. We have reason to believe he is dead."

"If one of your own men couldn't handle this thing, how in hell do you expect me to?"

"Will you stop talking for a while and listen? That's all I ask."

Martin accepted another cigarette. "Go ahead."

"While I'm talking to you, you are being cleared, that's how much confidence I've got that you'll accept. At Park Hill there are five research teams, each independent of the others. All are working on top secret programs. One of these projects is under the direction of Dr. Penn. His is one of the most important tasks ever undertaken by a scientist, let alone a man. Do you know what it is?"

"All I know," Martin said, "is that Dr. Penn won the Nobel Prize for research on cells and that he is now concerned with some phase of that for the army and that I'm supposed to do a cover story about him. The decision was made by the New York office. That's a laugh."

"Go ahead and laugh," the general said. "But the fact remains we're not pushing civilian institutions around just to please our fancy. There's a reason for it.

"Dr. Penn happens to be working on regeneration. He is trying to grow new arms and legs on men for ones that are destroyed. From the military standpoint perhaps that doesn't seem vital at the moment, since the military forces are so bent on destroying rather than creating. But in the long view, if Dr. Penn succeeds, it will be a tremendous boost for morale and our soldiers will be better fighting men than ever, for they will be able to fight fearlessly, always confident that if they are wounded and lose a limb a new one can be grown to replace it."

Martin grunted. "How about a dead soldier? I've seen many of them. Will this bring them back to life?"

The general snorted. "Very funny. Of course not. But it may be that someday Dr. Penn will have the solution to that, too. Who knows? He's a brilliant man. Think of what it would mean to have no more basket cases, no more armless or legless veterans. The procedure can later be turned over to civilian doctors. It may eventually offer hope to people who are now wearing wooden legs and arms and working springs and levers for fingers."

"Well, it's interesting," Martin said. "I can't deny that. It is a good thing, too. But where does *National Scene* come into the picture?"

"Some time ago it was brought to our attention by Colonel Sherrington, commanding officer at Park Hill, that valuable records of certain experiments carried over a long period of time were reported lost or stolen. Laboratory equipment that took months to make was found broken as if accidentally. It was more than mere coincidence. The colonel asked us to find out if someone just didn't want Penn Project, as it is called, to succeed."

"You mean he thinks someone is trying to keep the project from being completed?"

"Exactly. It's puzzling because it is actually a humane project with the eventual discoveries to be shared with all the nations of what we hope will be a grateful world."

"It would only be an insane man who would interfere with work of that nature," Martin declared.

"That's what we thought. A routine check was made by military police at Park Hill. They questioned Dr. Penn, the five research scientists and the twenty technicians he has working for him on the project. They made no progress.

"Three months ago, unknown to Dr. Penn or anyone else connected with the project, one of our men was sent. Forrest Killian went to work at Park Hill as a laboratory technician with Penn Project under civil service.

"Forrest Killian was a shrewd, careful man; he had been with the CIC for many years. He worked there for two weeks before communicating with me. He then said he didn't think anyone on the project could have hindered it, adding that he had made a complete and exhaustive study of the whole situation. He said the men were more than interested in their work. They worked long hours and talked of nothing else away from the laboratory.

"We were satisfied and the next time he called we were going to take him off the case and mark it up to coincidence after all. But he called up one night from the camp soon afterward and said he had been misled and that he had discovered someone who was hamstringing the work. Who do you suppose it was?"

"Dr. Penn."

The general's eyebrows shot up in surprise. "How did you guess?"

"In all the stories I read it's always the one you least suspect."

"You may have something there. It's true in this case, anyway. Mr. Killian said he suspected Dr. Penn and I asked him why. He said he didn't have time to explain over the phone but that he would let me know all about it after he confronted the doctor with the evidence."

"What happened?"

"We never heard from Forrest Killian again. That was a month ago. He disappeared, an impossible thing to do at Park Hill. You can't get on or off the reservation without going through the single gate and being subjected to the closest examination. A search was instituted, but there was no trace of him. They went over every square inch of the camp. We've been biting our fingernails here ever since. We know the guilty man but we cannot move against him."

They sat there for a while, neither saying anything. It was a respectful silence, as if it were for the missing agent.

"Stop me if I'm wrong," Martin said finally. "You want to get close to Dr. Penn to study him and try to learn what it was this Forrest Killian evidently found out about him, but you don't know how to do it through your own organization. So you conceive the brilliant idea of sending a writer to do his life story."

The general cleared his throat. "Let me put it this way, Mr. Enders. Dr. Penn would be suspicious of any new technician. If he and those in league with him have any organization at all, we could get no place through the regular channels. It has to be something unusual. Every man is susceptible to flattery, so the man who went to see him to write his success story would, we hope, catch him off guard."

The general opened a locked drawer, took out a sheaf of correspondence, plopped it on the table. "If it will help any, take a look at these. They are directives from the President himself giving priority to Penn Project."

Martin took him at his word, did not examine the papers.

"All who know about it feel regeneration is a humane project," the general continued. "Perhaps it is our collective conscience talking. But it would be earth-shaking if we did accomplish what we set out to do. If there is someone hampering it, we ought to know who and why. Don't you think regeneration would be a fine thing?"

Martin nodded. "Yes, of course it would be very worth

while. I can't see why anyone would want to sabotage it—especially the man directing the research on it."

"Exactly. It's a puzzler all right."

"You went to *National Scene* and convinced them they ought to send someone to do this story. Is that right?"

"Yes. They were very co-operative. I went right to Eldon D'Orsey, the editor in chief himself. He is the only one besides you who knows what this is all about."

"Some have their suspicions something is up."

"Really?"

"Nothing serious. But look: Am I supposed to do the story or not? I'm an unknown quantity as a criminal investigator; I'm afraid I wouldn't know where to begin."

"We don't want you to be a criminal investigator. Be a writer. All we want you to do is to go to Park Hill and be the most interested, the most inquisitive reporter you can. Go through the motions of writing his life story. We can't ask you to do anything else. But I would like it if you would follow up any leads that look suspicious and report back to me what you find out."

"And we never use the story, I suppose?"

The general gathered up the papers and put them back in the drawer. "If our suspicions prove correct, you may have quite a story yet, though it won't be the kind you planned. Otherwise, the story just never sees print. Mr. D'Orsey agreed to it that way."

"I ought to warn you, General Deems, that my interests don't run along these lines. I'm more interested in national affairs. I like to write stories that help create friendly international relations. Maybe I'm daft on that point, I don't know. If I am, maybe the war made me that way. But it is obvious this involves humanity and progress. If someone is deliberately standing in the way of this thing, I think he should be identified and made to account for it. So I'll go along with you. What are your instructions?"

The general beamed. "I knew you'd do it, Mr. Enders. So did Mr. D'Orsey."

# 4

Dr. Penn returned to his office, spluttering and lighting a new pipe from the desk as he sat down behind it.

"Grown men," he said. "That's what they are. Every one of the five. And not one of them can follow an order." He used the lighted pipe to emphasize his remarks by shaking it at Martin. "That's the trouble with scientists. They're all too temperamental. Always wanting their own way. Too long out of school. Where would they be today if they hadn't done what their teachers told them to do?"

Martin felt helpless before the doctor's wrath. He could only listen, watch the dancing eyes, the flush of anger on the cheeks. The doctor's pipe had gone out with the gesturing and he had to light it again.

"Take that Dr. Merrill. I suppose you are already aware by my talk with him on the phone that he and I don't see eye to eye. He wants to work his way and I want him to work mine. Co-operation! That's what we need. If each of the five was to do something different we'd never get anything done. Sometimes I think it would be better if I got rid of them all and did the work myself. At least then I'd know it was being done right."

Finally the anger died and the doctor looked at him and smiled. "Now I feel better, Mr. Enders. Didn't mean to make you suffer through it. But I feel better when I blow off a little steam once in a while. God knows I can't do it in front of them or they'd all quit. That would be a fine kettle of fish. Where were we?"

"You were telling me something about regeneration," Martin said. "But before you continue, I want you to know I stepped over to the window for a while. I couldn't help seeing those pictures on your desk."

"Virginia and Bobby?" The big man picked up the pictures, smiled affectionately at them. "Of course you'd want to know about them. Virginia is my daughter. She does most of the statistical work at the laboratory. She's very careful, very thorough. I'd like you to say she takes after her father, but there's more of her mother there, really. She'll be twenty-three soon."

"That other picture your son?" Martin Enders asked.

Dr. Penn nodded. "Bright lad. He's seven. His mother died when he was born. He'll be a scientist, I feel sure."

Martin made a few notations in his notebook. "What's he interested in, Doctor?"

"Bobby?" He pursed his lips. "He's just a boy. The things a boy of seven is usually interested in. The cowboy movie stars. He sees them at the reservation movies. He likes to build things, too."

"Does he have any pets?"

"No. No, he hasn't. He had a pet rabbit I let him take out of the lab once. But he didn't take care of it and I had to put it back."

"Is he interested in magic?"

"Magic? No, I don't think so. I don't know if he even knows what the word means."

Martin clutched his notebook in his two hands, looked the doctor straight in the eye. This would be the way to do it, to find out about it directly. He would be able to tell something by the answer.

"Dr. Penn," Martin said slowly. "I saw Bobby this afternoon."

"Really?" The doctor was surprised. "I don't see how you could have. He was in school. Unless you mean you saw him when you looked out of the window here. He could have walked past."

"No," Martin said firmly. "I saw him as I was coming in. Just before three o'clock. I saw him do a very strange thing."

The doctor lit his pipe again, studied Martin out of the corner of his eye. "What was that?"

Martin explained how he had seen the red-hued sphere disappear and how the cat materialized and ran away. The doctor didn't seem disturbed. He merely sat there sucking his pipe, his hands folded across his chest. Martin could not determine by his expression just what the doctor was thinking. He sensed no emotion. His face was a blank.

When Martin finished, the doctor picked up the phone, called a number. "Will you have Bobby come to my office in the administration building right away?" Then he put the phone back.

"You will find, Mr. Enders," the doctor said calmly, "that you could not have seen such a thing."

The next few minutes were embarrassing for both men. Martin did not wish to proceed until the matter had been proved to the doctor's satisfaction. The doctor evidently had nothing to say since his integrity seemed suddenly at stake. They sat sharing small talk and smoking nervously.

At length the staccato of running feet came down the hall,

the door burst open and a child ran across the room to Dr. Penn. The boy entered his father's embrace.

"Bobby, lad, what have you been doing?"

"Just playing, Dad. I was listening to *Tornado Bill* when you called. Miss Winters made me turn it off. I ran all the way."

"Bobby," the doctor said. "I'd like you to meet a new friend of mine. Mr. Martin Enders. He works for a magazine."

The boy stood in the circle of the man's arms and turned to look at Martin. *There was no sign of recognition in his eyes.*

"Do you ever listen to *Tornado Bill?*" the boy asked.

"No, I'm afraid not, Bobby," Martin said, his mind in a whirl. This was the boy, but the boy surely should have remembered. Perhaps the glance had not been enough . . .

"Bobby," Dr. Penn said. The boy turned to him. "What have you been doing this afternoon?"

"After school?"

"What time did you get out?"

"Three fifteen. You know the time."

"You didn't leave earlier?"

The boy shook his head, troubled. Martin concluded Bobby was the most accomplished child liar he had ever seen.

"I saw you a little before three," Martin said gently.

"I didn't see you. Where were you? Were you in school? Sometimes we have visitors, but mostly from other parts of the camp. Would you like to come and see the school? Tomorrow?"

"I didn't see you at school. I saw you as I was coming along the walk from the east gate to the administration building. Shall I tell you what you were doing?"

The boy's eyes grew wide in wonder and there was a trace of fear in them. His mouth was slack.

"You had a red sphere and you were making it dance. You waved your arm and it disappeared. Then you closed your eyes and something whirled in the air and a cat fell to the ground and ran away. Then you turned and looked at me. You were frightened and ran away. Don't you remember that?"

The boy was alarmed now and clung to his father. "What does he mean, Daddy? Why does he say I did that? What does he *want?*"

"You'd better not say anything more, Mr. Enders," the doctor said firmly. "You can see you've got the boy all worked up."

"But I'm telling you, I did see him!"

"Mr. Enders. I don't know what your purpose is, but you obviously did *not* see the boy. Isn't that apparent?"

"Are you calling me a liar?"

"You can believe what you will. I cannot alter what you say you saw. It is up to you to do that. All I am saying is that the boy did not lie. You can tell that."

"I tell you——"

"Don't let him do anything to me, Daddy!"

*"Mr. Enders!"*

Martin collapsed in his chair, letting the fury go out of him. It had been ridiculous to get so worked up. He was unfamiliar with children. The boy just didn't want to let his father know he played hookey from school. Perhaps it had been a bad thing to bring it up at all. He hoped he had not alienated the father who now held the child's head to his breast, stroking his hair. Martin had thought the recitation of what he had seen and the admission of them by the boy would lead to a useful development. Now he was stymied. He had played a high card and had lost.

"I'm sorry," Martin heard himself saying. "I was sure it was this boy. It must have been someone else."

"That's better." The doctor lifted the boy's head from his chest, looked into his eyes. "Mr. Enders is mistaken, Bobby. He only thought he saw you." The boy looked at Martin with mixed suspicion and fear. "I'm sure Mr. Enders will beg your pardon."

"I'm—I'm sorry, Bobby." He ground his teeth as he said it. The little imp. Has his father wrapped around his finger like adhesive tape. "I'm sorry, too, you had to miss *Tornado Bill* because of me."

"That's nice of you to say so, Mr. Enders." Dr. Penn patted his son's hair. "Better run along now, Bobby."

After the child had gone, Dr. Penn turned to him and asked, seriously, "Why did you do that, Mr. Enders?"

The father believed the boy. There was no sense in trying to convince him otherwise. "I was fully convinced he was the boy," Martin said, "until he denied it so emphatically. Now I see I must have made a mistake. It must have been another boy."

"But there are so few boys on the reservation!" Dr. Penn put up his hands in a gesture of despair. "I give up. You sounded so sure of yourself and Bobby never lies to me. I am only trying to find some reason for your acting as you did. You surprised me with your insistence."

"Let me say again I'm sorry, Dr. Penn. I only hope I haven't offended you. It wasn't exactly diplomatic of me to make such an issue of it; I'll try to behave myself from now on. Must be my nerves."

"Your business must be something like mine. Always on the go, always tense to some new situation. I sympathize with you. And while I think of it"—the doctor put his arms on the desk, leaned across it—"by putting you in that permanent barracks I'm making a technician out of you. That's where they all stay, the unmarried ones, that is. It wouldn't be polite for a guest to stay there. How would you like to stay at my house? It's not like home on the outside, there's no traffic in the streets in front of the house and you can't get delivery from the corner grocery, but you're welcome to stay. What do you say?"

"That's very nice of you, Doctor. I accept." Martin felt there was more to the invitation than mere courtesy. Was the doctor afraid now to have him mingle with the technicians? Or was he, Martin, just looking for ulterior motives? Perhaps it had been out of sheer politeness. He could not be sure.

The doctor glanced at his wrist watch. "It's after four. Might as well take you home, then. You can meet Ethel—that's the 'Miss Winters' Bobby mentioned, the housekeeper, chief cook and bottle washer—and Virginia will be home at five. Give you a chance to get moved in and settled down before dinner."

Building P-110 differed from P-108 and P-112 only in its occupants—the Penns. Otherwise the same windows faced the same street, the grass was trimmed the same height (Colonel Sherrington was very particular about the grass and was chauffeured around the camp periodically to inspect it), the cement walks to the front doors were all the same width. A small sign bore the message: "P-110 Dr. Eric Penn."

"All the houses along here have four bedrooms upstairs," Dr. Penn explained as they stepped out of the jeep and started up the walk. "It's a luxury not found on the outside. The army evidently expects its officers and civilian research workers to have large families. We are very comfortable in it, actually." As an afterthought, he added, "I hope you haven't worried that you'd be putting us out."

Martin wasn't worried about where he was going to sleep. He was worried lest his staying at the doctor's house meant the doctor wanted him under surveillance. He should get close to the doctor for *National Scene,* but if he were to do anything for General Deems he was going to have to get out on his own at least part of the time.

If there was any motive other than a feeling of genuine hospitality on his part, the doctor gave no evidence of it. He was a gracious and considerate host. He introduced him to Ethel Winters, an aging but still obviously efficient maiden lady who gave him a quick glance, gauged his appetite and hurried back to the kitchen to put some more beef in the stew.

The doctor showed him the guest room and suggested he make himself at home in it and then left him to his own devices while he ran a tubful of water down the hall and sang in an off-key voice.

Martin put his coat and hat in the closet, looked in the dresser mirror to comb his hair, then took a look out the window. It was a view such as one might get in a suburban neighborhood. Unusual for an army camp, except this wasn't fundamentally an army camp. The army boys were just the guards, the security people. Martin was used to an airfield with roaring planes and a big hangar and beacon lights.

When he turned around he was surprised to see Bobby standing in the doorway, looking at him curiously. The boy turned away.

"Hey, wait. Don't go."

The boy hesitated, came back, leaned against the doorjamb, looking at him hostilely now.

"How's Tornado Bill?" Martin threw him a smile to let him know all was forgiven, I don't care what you did, let's forget it.

"He won't be on till tomorrow."

"If I'm around will you let me listen with you?"

The eyes lighted with interest, then faded. "You wouldn't like him. Grown people don't like him. Even Daddy doesn't like him."

"I'll bet!" Martin laughed. "What are you going to be when you grow up? Another Tornado Bill?"

The boy shook his head. "I'm going to have a factory. I'm going to make rocket ships and repair everything. I'll bet I could make a rocket ship as big as this house. Bigger than Tornado Bill's *Jupiter Express*."

"No kidding?"

"You don't think I could, I bet."

"I wouldn't doubt it," Martin said casually. "I've seen you do some strange things."

"I will have lots of men working for me," the boy continued without giving any sign. "I'll have lots of money that people will give me and when we go I'll pick all the people I want to go with me."

"Could I go?"

"You'd be scared."

"Think so? I don't think I would be if you piloted the ship. The man who builds the ship ought to know how to run it."

The boy thought this over. Before he could speak again Martin asked him, "One thing I would like to know, Bobby, is why you didn't tell the truth in your father's office this afternoon. You know I saw you when I was walking this afternoon."

"But I *was* telling the truth," the boy said dismally. "How could you see me when I was in school?"

Martin gave up. "It must have been your twin brother, then." He made a mental note to check on the teacher.

The boy shook his head. A door slammed downstairs.

"That's my sister," he said. "You'll like her. Everybody does. Come on."

The memory of the photograph stirred Martin with a desire to see the girl and he was amazed at the eagerness with which he followed the boy across the hall and down the stairs.

"Hey, Sis!" Bobby cried. "A man's going to stay here!"

Martin laughed to himself as he wondered what this remark would mean to a beautiful twenty-three-year-old girl everybody liked, including Martin if the picture was a fair sample.

The floor of the hallway gave him only a glimpse of the lower floor as he descended the stairs behind Bobby. The first thing he saw was a pair of black pumps, a set of shapely ankles and nicely turned legs. Another few steps gave proof that the picture conveyed only a flat image of what was without question the most beautiful girl he had ever seen.

Their eyes met and held. She had evidently opened a letter and was reading it before she turned her head to see what manner of man it was her brother was shouting about. Martin did not trust his feet. He stopped mid-stairs and gaped. There was something electric there in the glance, something that touched a tender place within him. Her blush was contagious.

"I—I'm Martin Enders," he said.

"I'm 'Sis,' as Bobby said. Only my name's Virginia." Her voice was low, vibrant and sincere. She smiled warmly.

"Aren't you coming down?" Bobby asked impatiently.

"Ah—yes." Martin came down the rest of the stairs. "Bobby says everybody likes you, Virginia," he said in recovery. "Any truth in that?"

"Bobby's sweet," she said. "I'm afraid he sees in others only himself."

"Oh, I don't know. I can see why he'd say it."

"It's refreshing to meet someone gallant. Is it a characteristic of writers?"

"Not at all. I'm the only gallant one left. The others are all either happily married or turned recluse and live in caves hating all of civilization. But how did you know I was a writer?"

"Dad mentioned you were coming to interview him. Let's go into the living room. We can sit there." When they were moving, she said, "I think it's grand of *National Scene* to take such an interest in Dad. He's worked hard all his life."

He offered her a cigarette and as he lighted it for her, her eyes met his again. Closer, they did have an ethereal look, a misty quality that enhanced them. He had never seen eyes like hers before—challenging, provocative, exciting and curious, yet somehow reserved and cool.

"Tell me about your work," she said, blowing the smoke prettily. "It must be fascinating."

"At moments like this I agree."

"The unswervable gallant." She laughed. "But seriously, Dad did say he had been mentioned as a possible cover story. Will he be, do you think?"

"It all depends on what I find out," Martin answered.

"For example."

"Oh, the little things in his life that have made him the man he is. The things that made the turning points, the signposts along the way. I'm counting on you to help me out."

"I'll be glad to, Martin," she said agreeably. "Dad's apt to be pretty modest about some of the things he's done."

"He said he'd be hard to talk to. Said he was pretty busy with his project."

"It hasn't been going too well, frankly. He's been working very hard and there have been some upsets."

"Anything wrong?"

"Little things." As she sat there, her eyes looked far away and Martin wondered what she was thinking.

"How long has he been working on the project?"

"Nearly a year. He came here upon invitation of the government. He was head of the department of biology at Billingsley before this. There he had his own laboratory and lots of endowments. I think he misses the work. Government employment is so strenuous and you always have to account for everything and there are so many records—it's just too much for one man. It's not at all like Billingsley when Mother was living. She was devoted to Dad."

She was visibly affected, paused to control herself. "When she died he just literally immersed himself in his work and wouldn't talk to anyone. He's come out of it now, though."

"He said you work in the lab, Virginia. What do you do?"

"Some of the routine things. The records. I'm in charge of the stock and supplies."

"You make it sound dull."

She laughed. "How much do you know about science and laboratories, Martin? Perhaps you think of it as most people do—a fascinating place where four or five bearded men with thick glasses are tensely waiting the outcome of some experiment. It's never been like that for us. It's a grind, a slow, monotonous, checking, testing, double-checking, evaluating and re-evaluating. There seldom is a movielike dramatic moment when some result is instantly apparent. Sometimes you can have the answer for days without even knowing it."

"It seems to me you're taking it too far the other way," Martin countered. "Doesn't anything exciting *ever* happen? Hasn't anything exciting happened since you've been here?"

She looked at him oddly for a moment. "Yes, something did. But it wasn't in connection with the actual research."

"What was it?"

"There was a man," she said. "A technician named Mr. Killian. He disappeared and everybody on Park Hill spent a whole day looking for him. He was never found. That was about a month ago."

"What happened to him?"

"Heavens, I don't know. One day he was here and the next day he wasn't."

"Where did this man work?"

"That is the peculiar part of it. He worked right in Dad's laboratory and lived with the rest of the bachelor technicians in the permanent barracks. He couldn't just have walked off the job. I mention it because you're sure to hear about it."

Martin put out his cigarette. "What does your father think happened to Forrest Killian? I mean, doesn't he have a theory or something?"

"Dad was the last person to see him alive. He doesn't know what happened to him either." She looked at him sharply. "How did you know his first name?"

"You told me, Virginia." Suddenly he knew he'd never be an efficient CIC man. The bottom dropped out of his stomach. He hoped he didn't show what a big error he had made.

"I didn't tell you his first name, Martin. I just called him Killian."

"But you did! Otherwise how would I know?"

"I don't know."

She looked at him in wonder.

Ethel came in to say dinner was ready.

# 5

Dinner at the Penn house was a one-sided affair conversationally. Martin had counted rather heavily on extracting a few facts from the doctor, but he only managed to get two questions asked, for it was Bobby who monopolized the conversation, reciting tales of his future conquests in the never-never land of rocket ships and space pirates.

Dr. Penn did not seem to mind. He was occupied with his own thoughts as he methodically ate his meal, sometimes staring off into space as Bobby rattled on. He grunted monosyllabic answers to the child's questions.

Virginia smiled at Bobby's obvious penchant for incredible invention and imagery; the lad's enthusiasm and occasional gestures frequently made her laugh. This only led the child into even more startling adventures which he related with excited bright eyes and nonstop tongue.

It was Ethel, her dull grey hair sweeping straight back to a bun on her neck and her slate grey eyes coolly watchful of the boy's table manners, who kept interrupting the lad and telling him to eat.

"What's got into you tonight, Bobby?" Ethel said finally. "You don't have to impress Mr. Enders. You can tell him about your space adventures some other time."

Martin thought it was odd that the doctor and his daughter did not enforce Ethel's suggestion, especially when she looked at them as if seeking support for her action. When they did not return the look, she turned to Martin as if expecting him to make some comment.

He decided to take no notice of it. Besides, he had sensed through her cool and indifferent glances that she did not relish setting an extra plate for him and he did not want to alienate her. Instead, he told her he liked the stew. He was pleased to see her brighten. She had a vulnerable spot.

"Virginia and I have some work to do in the laboratory," Dr. Penn said after dinner while he was filling his corncob. "The work is a bit strenuous and we'd have no time to talk to you, Martin. I suggest you go to an area movie. You can come to the lab tomorrow."

"We always get the films before Avon Ridge," Virginia said. "Sometimes even months before."

"I'm afraid I don't care much for movies," Martin said

truthfully. "I would prefer staying right here and waiting for you to get back."

"We may be quite late." The doctor and his daughter exchanged glances. "You had better go."

"I'd prefer just wandering about the area, if you don't mind."

"It would be dangerous to go poking around," the doctor said. "Somebody might get the wrong idea and take a shot at you. Here's where the movie is." He picked up a scrap of paper and drew a diagram. "To get to it, you've got to go down these streets. Here we are; this is where the movie is."

Martin felt color rising in his neck. "I told you I don't like movies. I go only once or twice a year. Why do you insist I do something I don't want to do?"

"Mr. Enders," the doctor said, his grey eyes glittering, "you do want to stay out of trouble, don't you?"

"But I don't see——"

"Dad's right, Martin. You don't know the reservation very well. The movie would be the best thing to do your first night here."

In the end, to avoid a quarrel he could not afford, he thanked the doctor for the diagram and left the house.

He had no intention of going to a movie.

He found the acceptable streets were the ones with people on them. He stayed on these, passing regulation army buildings and other more bizarre structures probably built for some specific bit of research. These bore the legend: "Authorized Personnel Only." He did not argue.

The streets reminded him of a carnival, for every square inch of ground was brightly illuminated as at a midway. Through these avenues moved military police cars bearing armed men in uniform who were alert and efficient-looking. Every once in a while such a vehicle would stop a group and the white-gloved MP's would ask to see identification cards.

"You're out of Area One, buddy," a sergeant who took a look at his ID card told him at one point. "Better get back where you belong."

Martin's wanderings brought him at length to a single-story structure from which was coming the sound of many voices, laughter and the blare of a jukebox. He looked in. It was crowded, but he saw a vacant table on the far side of the room. He pushed his way through couples on the dance floor, bought a bottle of beer at the counter and made his way to the table. He sat there for a while, wondering if all the people there worked on Penn Project, when he noticed an older man standing at the end of the counter looking at him.

The man eventually made his way across the floor to Martin's table.

"Are you alone?" he asked. When Martin nodded, he said, "I saw you come in. I figured maybe you'd want company. I hate sitting at a table all by myself and thought maybe you did, too. Not expecting anybody, are you?"

Martin told him to sit down, offered him a cigarette when the man had drawn up a chair, depositing his glass and bottle on the table.

"Don't smoke," the man said. "Gave it up a couple years ago. You're new around here, aren't you?" The eyes were dull beneath the high forehead, the salt and pepper hair. His glasses needed cleaning and his breath smelled of something stronger than beer.

"Just arrived today," Martin said.

"Hey, Cholly!" The voice came from the doorway and they both turned to see three young fellows headed their way. "Hey, we're late, Cholly," one of them said, coming over. "Your offer still good?"

"You apes know I never made any offer," Martin's partner said. "But sit down. I've never been known to refuse to buy a drink."

"Amen," another said as the three drew up chairs.

"Three over here!" the third man yelled to the counterman.

"I'd introduce you to these simpletons, but I don't know your name."

"I don't know yours either."

"You don't know Dr. Charles Merrill?" one of the youths said in amazement. "Why, you told us you were famous in the outside world, Doctor."

"You can turn it off," Dr. Merrill said. "This is Karl Gronemeier—the loud one—and Amos Page and Chalmers Peterson."

"My name is Enders. Martin Enders."

All four stared.

"I'll be damned!"

"We heard about you."

"Yeah. You're better known than Dr. Merrill."

"At least Dr. Penn knows *you're* living, Mr. Enders. The doc here can't say as much."

They all laughed, poured their beer.

"All right, leeches," the doctor said. "Drink this damned three-point-two. A man can't raise a thirst around here, Mr. Enders. There's nothing but this sarsaparilla to quench it with."

"You do better than that, Doc."

"Wait a minute," Martin broke in. "How come you fellows know about me?"

"You're strictly FGSDTHA, that's what," Amos said. "You don't look that bad, either."

"All right," Martin said. "I'll bite. What's the alphabet for?"

"Ah. That, sir," Dr. Merrill explained, "means you're a member of the select and exclusive organization known as the For God's Sake Don't Tell Him Anything Club. It's popular on this reservation."

"Orders from headquarters," Karl said.

Chalmers chuckled. "He means Dr. Penn."

"I take it Dr. Penn told you men to say nothing to me if I questioned any of you. Is that right?" Martin asked.

The heads nodded. "Nothing. Absolutely nothing."

"That doesn't mean we can't ask *you* questions," Dr. Merrill said. "For example, what are you doing here?"

"I'm doing a cover story for *National Scene* on Dr. Penn."

"We don't get anything out of him," Karl said. "What makes you think you'll do any better?"

There was laughter at this.

"They're right," Dr. Merrill said. "If he's as close-mouthed about his past with us, how are you going to learn anything?"

"That," Martin said, pouring the last of his beer into his glass, "is exactly what *I* would like to know."

"He carries it too far," the doctor said. "Frankly, this whole business of security makes me sick. You'd think we were trying to invent another atomic bomb or something. We're not. If we were near reaching the end of our research, there'd be a reason for it. But not now. Hell, we're not even started yet. Oh, for the lab with no restrictions, with no Dr. Penn to interfere!"

"Does he interfere?" Martin ventured. "I'd think he'd want to get it over with as fast as possible so he could get on with something else."

"You don't know Dr. Penn," Karl said. "Sometimes it's not actually interfering, it's *not* doing something. Did you ever work in a factory, Mr. Enders?"

"No."

"Well, if you had, you'd know there is such a thing as a suggestion box. You drop in a suggestion and, if it's a good one, you get a cash award. They do the same thing here. You make a suggestion and you put it in the box. Then Dr. Penn takes it and reads it and studies it and maybe he even sleeps on it all night. Then the next day——"

"The next day," Amos cut in, "he throws it in the wastebasket."

" 'Suggestion'? What suggestion?"

There was laughter again. Loud laughter.

"You parasites have had my offering for the evening," Dr. Merrill said, getting up. "I'll leave you now. I might interfere with your technique. An old man would be in the way."

"Go on, we might interfere with yours."

"Who's the dame?"

"Where do you keep her, Doc?"

"He sneaks up to her room every night."

Dr. Merrill turned to Martin. "I'm offering you a chance to get away from these bums, Mr. Enders. Better take it."

"I think I will," Martin said. "But I'll make my contribution. I'll buy you fellows one before I leave."

"Hey, he's a real white guy."

"He doesn't act like a writer."

"Come around later, Mr. Enders. Always room for a live one."

"They're good kids," Dr. Merrill said when they were outside. "They're just fed up with Park Hill. Hell, we all are. How would you like to be cooped up here for a month at a time? Let's go where we can talk. Are you staying at P-4?"

"No. I'm staying with Dr. Penn," Martin answered.

"Dr. Penn!" He whistled. Then he looked closely at Martin. "Are you sure you're staying there?"

"Dr. Penn asked me to. Is there a rule against it or something?"

Dr. Merrill shook his head in wonder. "No. Let's see; you just got in today, didn't you?"

Martin nodded.

"Then you haven't spent a night there yet."

"What are you driving at?"

"Let's got to my place. I'm in P-4. It's right down the street."

In his small room on the second floor of a brick barracks, Dr. Merrill reached into the rear of a dresser drawer and brought out a bottle of whisky.

"I didn't think you could get that at a place like this," Martin said.

"I couldn't, ordinarily. Got this on prescription from the section pharmacy. For my heart." He chuckled. "Besides, I know somebody over there. Have a drink?"

"Never use it while I'm working."

"You working now?" Dr. Merrill pulled out the stopper, gave him a sharp look. "You working for Dr. Penn by any chance?"

"I don't follow you. Here's my card." Martin showed him his *National Scene* press card.

To Martin's surprise, Dr. Merrill took the card, ran his fingers over it, looked at it toward the light, then handed it back. Evidently satisfied, he poured himself a half tumbler of whisky and, since Martin was seated in the only chair, moved to the bed and settled himself on it. He took a drink, sighed contentedly. "That's more like it. Now, if you're not working for Dr. Penn, how come you're staying there?"

"It's just as I said. He asked me. You seem to think there's something wrong in staying there."

"Dr. Penn never does anything without a purpose. I'm merely trying to figure out why he would want you there."

"Frankly, I've wondered about the same thing," Martin admitted. "First, he made arrangements for me to stay there. Then, for some reason, he changed his mind. He changed it right after he talked with you this afternoon."

"After he talked with me?" The doctor looked at him with suspicion. "How do you know about that?"

"I was in his office when you called him."

"Mmm." The doctor downed the rest of the glass, turned it in his fingers while he looked at it. "Why should *National Scene* be interested in Eric Penn? Can you answer that?"

"He's a famous scientist. He's done a lot for humanity. Nobel prizewinner. We've run stories about men who have done less."

"I suppose his research in annelids is a classic." Dr. Merrill put his glass on the floor. "He's lived with trichina so long he can call them all by their first names. Yes, I can't deny he's recognized as an authority on cytology, embryology and genetics."

"Then what are you getting at?"

"You heard the boys talking, Martin. Hell, Dr. Penn is running this project as if he were bossing a corporation. He's not conducting research."

"What's he doing that's wrong?"

"He's lost his Arrowsmith mind, for one thing." The doctor got up from the bed for a fresh drink. Martin wondered how he could see his way around through his smudgy glasses. He brought the full glass back to the bed with him and sat with it. "He knows better. You can't paint according to formula and have art; you can't compose music by the numbers. Science is just as much a creative art. You've got to go where you have a hunch you should go. You've got to follow your inspirations. You have to be daring, adventurous. Want to know why I think he wants you at his house?"

"Sure. Why?"

Dr. Merrill finished his drink, lay on the bed, put his hands behind his head, looked up from the pillows to the lone, harsh light bulb in the ceiling, squinting his eyes thoughtfully.

"We've all felt it," he said. "You're just another example of it. For some reason he doesn't want you to ask questions. If you're at his place you won't be learning anything from us. That's why he told us all about you today." The doctor sat up, loosened his tie. "What would you think of a man who insists you do research *that has already been done?*"

"He does that? Don't you point that out to him?"

Dr. Merrill snorted. "Sure. He just smiles. 'Maybe they didn't do it right before,' he says. Now I ask you: What kind of an answer is that?"

"Why should he stand in the way of his own project, then?"

"You're asking me!" The doctor laughed. He seemed to think it was a huge joke. "Don't you suppose we all wonder? How would you like working in a situation like that? The result is nobody gives a damn any more. Nobody cares what goes on. The project is marking time." The doctor disregarded the glass, got the bottle and took a nip from it every now and then. "It's all as if we're in prison, that's what it is, see? There's no escape. You have to stay your time out, see? And I've signed up for three years." He chuckled and his movements were deliberate and slow; his eyes were burning now as if with fever.

"I've got a good record," the doctor went on. "Oh, I know school research isn't a bed of roses. You bet your bottom dollar it isn't. You've always got a class to teach jus' when you come to the climax, but at least you're makin' progress. You're movin' somewhere, see? You're coverin' ground, that's what you are. You're not markin' time. See what I mean?" He gestured with the bottle and the liquid sloshed around inside it.

"Doesn't anybody have a theory about it?"

"Hell, *everybody's* got a theory! Some think he's goin' off his rocker. Some think he's workin' for Russia. Me? I got a little theory all of my own and I'll be damned if I'll tell you." He squinted his eyes and tried to keep them on Martin. "At least I'll never tell you while you're stayin' at Dr. Penn's house. That's how it is. If you were stayin' here——"

"Does Dr. Penn ever act in a peculiar way?"

"He's a peculiar guy all the time, he is."

"I mean, does he ever do anything out of the way?"

"Lettin' us do what we want would be that," he said thickly.

"How about his daughter, Virginia?"

The doctor took a swig, wiped his mouth with the sleeve of the arm holding the bottle. "You know about her, then. Well, I guess you'll be knowin' more about her as time goes on. Give you a couple of days, Mart, m'boy. It'll take jus' a couple days." His head was lolling drunkenly.

"And his son, Bobby? What about him?"

"We're all lonely, see? That's what I mean. Lonely. Nobody loves us. Except maybe Virginia. You seen Virginia? Sure you have. Just said so, didn't you? Good ol' Virginia. What a gal! How can a man like that have a daughter like that! I'm askin' you. She's a dream girl." This struck him funny and he started to laugh.

"How about Forrest Killian?" Martin asked in a voice loud enough to interrupt the laughter.

"Who?" The doctor goggled at him.

"Forrest Killian."

"Forres' Killian. Killian. Oh, him! He stuck him in a test tube."

"Test tube!"

"Might as well have. Forres' was a nice fella. Kinda like you. Y'know? He was up here lots. Here, have another."

Martin took the bottle, then handed it back without drinking.

"Why do you say he might as well have been stuck in a test tube?"

"Lemme have a cigarette."

Martin gave him one, had difficulty in following the weaving head to light it for him.

"About the test tube," Martin prompted.

"It's this night, see?" The doctor waved the cigarette around. "This night Forres' goes to Dr. Penn's office. Wha' happens? Does he ever come out?" He shook his head. "No. Only Dr. Penn comes out and he locks his office as he always does and would he lock a nice fella like Forres' in his office? I'm askin'. Would he now?"

"No, he wouldn't do a thing like that."

"Where did he go, then? Where did he go? He never came out. Must have stuck him in a tes' tube. Print that in your ol' magazine."

"Does Dr. Penn have laboratory equipment in his office?"

The doctor shook his head groggily. "No, but he might as well have for all the good it's doin'. We're all workin' on nothin'. Forres', order the burettes. We gotta titrate this right, see? Don' lose that nucleus, that may be the one. Hey, who broke the glass? Somebody'll get hell; that took months to make. Don't tell me, let me guess. Want to know who busted it? I'll tell you because I kinda like you. *Dr. Penn broke it himself!*"

The doctor belched and shook his head. "You found out, didn't you, Forres'? Don' tell him. Don' go into his office. I told you, remember? Don' go. *Don' go!*" The doctor was slobbering now and he was crying. The bottle dropped out of his hand and hit the floor, the liquid left in it spilling along the floor as it rattled across the boards. The doctor suddenly collapsed on the bed.

Martin undressed the man, put him to bed, turned out the light and left the barracks. Whether or not Dr. Penn and his daughter had returned from the laboratory, Martin had no way of knowing; except for the night lights, the house was dark when he entered it.

In his room, he undressed and went to bed, only to lie there thinking of his cover story and his duty toward the CIC.

How can I pretend to write about Dr. Penn as a man of scientific stature when his scientific logic is questioned by his fellow workers? How can I appear to be building up a man with one hand while I'm trying to knock him down with the other? Dr. Merrill has given me a start with this nonsensical test-tube business, but it might be just the mouthings of an alcoholic . . . What did he say, though, about staying at the Penn house?

Perhaps Dr. Penn's mind has snapped. After all, it would take a crazy man to stop a humanitarian project like regeneration. If his errors are so obvious to his fellow workers, maybe he is or has gone off the deep end. But what about Forrest Killian? How to explain him? And there is that incident with Bobby to explain.

He went to sleep reliving the experience. There was this red sphere and it kept dancing up and down and up and down . . .

*. . . Except it wasn't really a sphere. It was Dr. Penn's head. The head gave a polite little cough.*

*"I quite agree with you," Dr. Penn said from his place at the foot of the bed. He leaned on the bed railing, his head resting on his arms. "But you haven't told me everything."*

*"Now how did you know that?" Martin asked. "I tried to keep it a secret."*

*"Somebody else tried to do that once. Virginia said you mentioned Forrest Killian's name. Did you know him?"*

*Martin shook his head, drew the covers closer about his shoulders. "Never met him. General Deems told me about him."*

*"Good old General Deems. Where is he now?"*

*"At his office in Washington."*

*"Is he interested in Mr. Killian?"*

*"Not only interested, he's befuddled." Martin laughed. It was silly for them to be talking about Forrest Killian like that. The general certainly wouldn't have liked it.*

*Dr. Penn chuckled. "You have a sense of humor, haven't you, Martin? You and I, we'll get along all right." He paused to materialize a pipe already lit. "As I understand it, it's your job to find out what happened to Forrest Killian, as well as to get a story on me for* National Scene. *Is that right?"*

*"Right as rain." Odd way of saying it, but it was the correct thing to say to Dr. Penn. "The story's just a cover-up."*

*"What did you do tonight?"*

*"I talked to several of your technicians and Dr. Merrill."*

*"Dr. Merrill? Oh, that's bad. You probably got all you could out of Dr. Merrill, didn't you?"*

*Martin laughed. "He got drunk as hell. He told me how you put Forrest Killian in a test tube." Martin roared. This was funny. Imagine someone you didn't even know being in a test tube!*

*"Really? Tell me about it." The doctor was interested.*

*The doctor accidentally dropped his pipe and it hit the floor with a rap.*

Martin awoke with a start and sat up in bed in a cold sweat. His heart was beating like a jackhammer. He found himself looking frantically around the room, but the moonlight showed no one there.

What was wrong?

With a rush of remembrance he knew someone had been talking to him in a dream, asking him questions and that he was answering them. The memory of it was so keen he could remember the warmth and pleasure of it, but when he tried to visualize who it was he was talking to, he could not. The questioner in the dream—of course it was a dream—must have asked a vital question that spelled danger and tripped the mechanism that woke him before he could answer, just as one awakens with a start after he has jumped off a high building in a dream.

That was it. How silly of him, of his subconscious mind. But his hands were trembling.

# 6

Martin responded sluggishly to the knock on the door. When it was repeated, he got up on his elbows. "Yes?"

The door opened part way and Ethel stood there looking severe.

"Beg pardon, Mr. Enders," she said. "It's seven o'clock."

"Seven? That's early, isn't it?"

"Dr. Penn and Virginia have already had their breakfasts. The doctor wants to see you at the administration building at eight."

"What's up?"

"I don't know. How do you want your eggs?"

"Straight up, thanks."

He tried bounding out of bed when she had gone, but his leap lacked the vigor it should have. Immediately he knew why. The night had been spent half awake, listening, waiting for another visitation. In the brightness of the sunny morning the experience seemed unreal and he chided himself for having lost sleep over something so elusory. He found circles under his eyes when he looked at himself in the bathroom mirror and reproved himself again for his fears.

"The next thing you know," he said to himself, "you'll be believing in ghosts."

He ate his eggs at a place set for him in the kitchen.

"If you want more coffee," Ethel said, "you'll find it on the stove."

"You make me sound like a lazy, late-rising roomer, Ethel. Aren't you going to keep me company?"

"I have work to do," she said, stepping to the door of the room. "And I have to wake Bobby and get him ready for school."

"Wait. Sit down." When she looked at him in surprise, he added, "I didn't mean that the way it sounded. I just want to talk to you, that's all."

"And what am I supposed to do with my work?" Her eyes held the merest glimmer of anger.

"Did Dr. Penn tell you, too, not to talk to me?" he asked.

"He certainly did not. Why shouldn't I talk to you?"

"That's what I'm asking you." He shot her a smile and she relented, sitting then at the table.

"How long have you worked for Dr. Penn?"

"Ever since he came to Park Hill."

"You never saw him before that?"

"No. Why?" Her grey eyes were alarmed.

"Just trying to fill in his background. He told you I'm doing a story on him for *National Scene* didn't he?"

She nodded. "He mentioned it, but I didn't think you'd be asking me anything. I don't know anything about him."

"You know what he likes to eat. That would tell something about the man, wouldn't it? Our magazine tries to make its sketch of a man as complete as possible."

"Well, if you're going to put that in," Ethel said, "you can say he loves pot roast and noodles. Homemade noodles."

"The way Ethel Winters makes them, I'll bet."

"Well." The housekeeper-cook lifted her head with pride. "If I do say so, I've never tasted noodles like mine."

"Promise you'll make some for me sometime, will you?"

Ethel's eyes fairly glowed. She saw his cup was empty, poured him more coffee.

"How long has Dr. Penn been at Park Hill?"

"It was a year last month, Mr. Enders."

"Does he have any unusual habits?"

She looked away. "No. Except . . . well, Park Hill isn't like living anywhere else."

"Why did you look away, Ethel?"

Color seeped into her face and she drew her lips into a thin line. "It's nothing, Mr. Enders."

He had finished his eggs. He lit a cigarette and sipped his coffee. "Tell me about it," he said casually.

"There's nothing to tell. Really, Mr. Enders." Her voice quavered and held a note of dismay.

"Why are you so disturbed, Ethel?"

"I'm not disturbed," she said hastily. "If you don't hurry" —she waved toward the clock—"you'll be late. It's nearly eight now."

"But this is interesting. Much more interesting than keeping the appointment. You've got my curiosity aroused."

"It's nothing, believe me!" She was frightened now.

"Are you afraid I'll use it in the magazine? Is that it?"

"No!" she cried. Then her shoulders sagged. "It's that, that Dr. Penn—sometimes, the way he looks at me . . . I'd be afraid to say anything."

"Now isn't that just like a woman," he said, laughing. "Leading you on and then refusing to tell you anything."

"But I didn't lead you on. You only guessed——"

"There *is* something," he said calmly. "And you're going to tell it to me. You can trust me."

Ethel's eyes glittered and she bit her lower lip. "All right," she said at last. She got up, went into the dining room. Coming back, she closed the door between. She then went to the back door, opened it and looked out, seemed satisfied, then resumed her place at the table. She was trembling. She leaned toward him.

*"He doesn't sleep in his bed,"* she whispered.

"He doesn't sleep in his bed!"

Ethel nodded. Her face flushed, she went on, "He used to mess it up so I'd think he slept in it, but he doesn't any more. He doesn't bother."

Martin was puzzled. "Where does he sleep, then?"

"I don't know. I just don't know. And that's not all. Sometimes Virginia doesn't sleep in her bed either and once or twice Bobby . . . Oh!" She was suddenly distraught. "I don't know what to think. I don't *want* to think about it."

"But where could they all sleep? At the laboratory?"

"I don't know, Mr. Enders. But they all come home sometime during the night, or early in the morning before I get up. I've given up trying to make any sense out of it."

"Well, that *is* odd." Could the whole family have slept a time or two at the laboratory? Certainly they wouldn't want Bobby to do that, a mere child. But why didn't Dr. Penn ever sleep at home? Did he have a bed at the lab? It was a bewildering development.

"Something else, Mr. Enders. At first I was afraid I was losing my mind, but now I know I'm not. It's when you don't know you're going crazy that you go crazy, you know. So I'm not afraid."

"What is this other thing?"

"Well, after I had been here a few months I was putting the fresh ironing away. I had some of Dr. Penn's shirts to put in his dresser, so I walked upstairs to his room and the door was closed. I knocked, but there was no answer. So I walked in and put the shirts away. Dr. Penn was not in his room. I was sure of that.

"When I came out and closed the door, I stood there for a few minutes thinking about what I ought to do next. All of a sudden the door behind me opened and Dr. Penn came out. I screamed and the doctor wanted to know why. I told him he frightened me, that I didn't think he was in the house. I didn't tell him I was just in his room putting the shirts away."

Her eyes were big with wonder and she was almost breathless with the telling of it. "How do you account for that, Mr. Enders?"

"I don't know," he said. "What do you think of it?"

"I can't imagine," she said solemnly. "Dr. Penn must have climbed up the outside of the house. But at his age!"

"Do you think he suspects that you know?"

"He's never mentioned it. Do you think he does?"

Martin snubbed out his cigarette in his saucer. "Let me ask you another question. Do you sleep well?"

She blushed. "Of course I do. With all the work there is to do around here I'm dead tired at the end of the day."

"Have you always slept well since you came here?"

"Well, I have had my dreams. I've always had dreams, but never like the ones I've had since I've been here."

"What kind of dreams are they?"

Her color deepened. "They're silly. I always get scared afterward. I was so scared when I first started having them I thought of leaving."

"Tell me about them."

"Oh, I couldn't, Mr. Enders. Really."

It was a long shot. "Does somebody ask you questions when you're asleep?"

It hit the mark. Her mouth dropped open. "How—how did you guess? Say . . ." Her face blanched.

"No," he said reassuringly. "Don't be frightened. I only know because someone was asking me questions in my sleep last night."

"Dr. Penn?"

"I don't know. Could it have been?"

"It is with me. Only sometimes I dream about all three Penns. Just as if they were right in my bedroom with me and we're having a visit. At first I didn't remember the dreams but when they happened so often I began to remember what they were like. Do you think I *am* losing my mind, Mr. Enders?"

"No, I don't think so." He looked at the clock. It was 8:18. "I'd better go." He rose. "Look, let's keep this just between you and me. All right?"

"I won't tell another living soul, Mr. Enders."

"Where have you been?"

Dr. Penn shot the question the moment Martin opened the door to his office in the administration building. He was sitting behind his desk, his arms folded.

Martin could feel the informality he had expected withering and dying in the air of the room. There was an annoyed edge to the voice. Gone was the mildly bantering tones of the previous afternoon.

"People don't keep me waiting."

"I've been talking with Ethel," Martin replied truthfully, taking a chair. "She said you wanted to see me."

"What else did she have to say?"

Martin shrugged. "A few little essentials I might find useful in *National Scene,*" he said brightly. "Like your penchant for pot roast and noodles."

The tension lifted momentarily as the doctor rocked back in his squeaking chair, lighting his pipe. "She does make a fine pot roast. I'll say that for Ethel." He continued to rock, sucking his pipe, studying Martin through the clouds of smoke that always whirled around his head when he rocked and smoked at the same time.

"What," Martin ventured gently, "did you want to see me about? I thought I was to go to your laboratory this morning."

"You didn't go to the movie last night."

Martin sighed, kept the doctor waiting while he lit a cigarette and contributed to the haze of the room with a long plume of smoke.

"Why were you so insistent that I go, Doctor?"

"Damn it!" The chair rocked forward and the doctor's fists hit the desk. It made Martin jump. "I'm responsible for you, man! You are a guest of mine and if anything happened to you I would be held to blame."

"You mean like what happened to Forrest Killian?" It was worth taking a chance.

The doctor's grey eyes snapped and his short-cropped hair bristled. "So Dr. Merrill went through that, did he? What else did he tell you?"

"You're wrong, Doctor. It was your daughter who told me about Killian."

"But you're not denying you talked to Dr. Merrill!"

"Of course I talked to him," Martin snapped. "I'm not one of your technicians, you know. I'm a free agent."

"Not so free. Not so free. Not while you're here. You have to abide by reservation rules." His pipe had gone out and the doctor savagely struck a match on the underside of the desk, puffing vigorously at the pipe to get it started again.

"Do the reservation rules say I have to report to you my every action, where I am at every hour of the day?"

"There is no written rule. But the head of every research unit wants to know where his people are."

"But I'm not one of your people! I happen to be an associate editor of a magazine. I'm here to do you a favor, write you up for it." Martin thrust his cigarette into an ashtray. "I don't see why I should do the story on you at all, in the light of this development."

"I agree," the doctor said bluntly.

Martin looked at him carefully. A changeable, unpredictable man, the doctor. His reasoning was ulterior and hard to analyze. His eyes, his mouth with the pipe, the folded arms across the chest, the slight rock of the chair—none of it gave a clue to his logic.

"If that is the way you feel," Martin said slowly, "why did you approve of the story in the first place?"

"Originally I had some idea it might help the profession. I thought, too, it might inspire someone to enter research. I didn't think the magazine would send someone here to stay for a while—I was not prepared for that," the doctor answered.

"You didn't know I would be cleared for technical information either, did you?"

The doctor coughed. "That had nothing to do with it. It's—it's just that I can't spare the time, Mr. Enders."

"You should have said so yesterday. What's happened? Are you afraid I'll find out something terrible about you?"

"I suppose that's a joke," the doctor said, a bright curiosity behind his eyes. "The truth is I don't think you're good for morale. It hurts Dr. Merrill, for example, to think you are writing a story on me when he feels he has done as much for science."

"Dr. Merrill doesn't seem to mind."

"I suppose you're going to tell me he thinks it's great."

"No. He doesn't agree with you, that's all. He doesn't like the way you're running things. He thinks you're holding up your own project. Would you care to confirm or deny that?"

The doctor took a deep breath and a hot rush of angry blood darkened his face. The room itself seemed to sense the rising tide of resentment and Martin found the air hard to breathe. As suddenly as it came on, it was gone. The doctor drew the pipe out of his mouth, sent it skittering across the desk, leaned back in his chair and laughed. Then he came around the desk and sat on it, facing Martin, good humor in his face.

"This is ridiculous, Martin. Why does everybody think I stand in the way of my own project? It doesn't make sense, does it?"

"Not the way things stand right now," Martin said darkly. "It might if a reason could be discovered."

The doctor laughed again. When he stopped, he took Martin by the shoulder and led him out of the office. "Let's visit the laboratory," he said. "Then you can decide whether or not I'm stalling the project."

There was no way to tell that Building P-22 in the northeast sector of Park Hill Research Reservation was the regeneration research center. Like all the laboratories on the reservation, it was a single-story structure occupying an entire block, painted dead white and bearing the usual "Authorized Personnel Only" signs.

The thing that marked it apart from other smaller buildings about it was the opaque glass windows, standard equipment at the field for research centers. There were only two doors: one at either end.

When Martin and Dr. Penn slid up to it in the doctor's jeep, there was a workman cutting the grass around it.

"It isn't my idea of a laboratory," Dr. Penn said as they got out of the vehicle and started for the door. "This is the army's conception of one. But it is adequate."

The inside of the long, narrow structure was divided into two sections. One for the actual research, the other, at the opposite end, for Dr. Penn's office and the offices of the other resident scientists.

When they entered the lab end, Martin found himself surrounded by the usual laboratory sights and smells—retorts, animal cages, shelves of bottles, charts, assorted devices he could not name, and a faint odor of formalin, a trace of alcohol and ether. The technicians, who were busy at long tables, were wearing white smocks and Martin caught a glimpse of Dr. Merrill among them. The doctor did not look up.

"I hope you're not disappointed," Dr. Penn said. "We don't equip laboratories as they do in the movies. This is our working area. Back here we have our offices."

They walked through the wide aisles between equipment and lab tables to the corridor at the other end of the building.

"There are three offices on each side of the building here," the doctor explained. "Mine is here at the end. Dr. Merrill's is across the corridor."

Virginia, looking pert and efficient in her white smock, looked up as they came through the door, flashed a smile at Martin.

"Good morning," she said.

It had been nothing special, but the way she said it reaffirmed a feeling he had been having about her.

"Good morning," he returned, irked that he could think of nothing bright to say.

"If you don't mind, Virginia, Martin and I have something to talk over."

The girl excused herself and when she left, the doctor closed the door and motioned Martin to a chair while he unlocked a drawer and drew out a sheaf of papers.

"The secret of regeneration," the doctor said, seating himself in the desk chair and swiveling around with the papers on his knees, "is in the cell. The early cell. The embryonic cell. In the beginning there is rapid cell division. What determines what each cell is going to do? How does one know it is supposed to form part of the head or the arm? You see?"

Martin nodded, noticed that the walls of the room were covered with graphs, charts and diagrams. There were technical words and descriptions he did not understand. Biology was not one of his fortes.

"These papers," the doctor went on, "are records of experiments we have been carrying on. For your information, we are experimenting mostly on frogs, though there are the usual animals out there—hamsters, white rats, guinea pigs, rabbits. We're interested in frogs because a frog is unable to replace a limb but is able to regenerate one as a young tadpole. Why has he lost this power? This morphological repair—the restoring of the limb—is lost with adulthood because the special cells held in reserve for the purpose of restoring the lost parts as tadpoles undergo a differentiation. By that I mean they have specific tasks for an adult frog, but for a tadpole they are a plastic material, indifferent to what they may be called upon to form.

"These cells are created in layers of tissue which, since the development of the embryo, have not undergone any special alteration or else serve for purposes other than connecting different parts of the body.

"If a differentiated cell could undergo dedifferentiation, then we'd have the trick."

Martin frowned, trying to digest the information. "You mean if you could take a normal cell and make it into one of these regenerating cells, then you'd have the answer to growing an arm or a leg on a frog—or a man."

The doctor smiled. "Roughly, that's it. But how to change the cell? How can we get it to do what we want it to do? Why does a cell suddenly break away and start multiplying chaotically to form a cancer? Our purpose is very similar, except it must be in a definite direction."

"Dr. Merrill said you were doing research that had already been done. How about that?"

"Research is never done just once and never repeated,"

the doctor said patiently. "Would you look at the sky with a telescope and never look again? In a way, Dr. Merrill is right. Yes, we're doing research that has been done before. We're trying to find out, for example, what Spermann failed to discover: Why does a cell differentiate and forever lose its plasticity?"

The doctor tossed the papers to his desk, turned to get one of the Missouri meerschaums on the pipe rack.

"Dr. Merrill and the others have their own ideas. I am having them trace the growth of the egg cell of a frog. They think it's below them, that it's elementary. Well, I say it *is* elementary and the solution will be elementary when we find it. They have been instructed to be very particular and exhaustive. They are all doing the same thing. It makes me angry to think they feel they are wasting their time."

He lit the pipe and puffed on it furiously. "If they don't discover something new, then we'll take the adult frog, cut off its leg and put in its place an undifferentiated cell. Then we'll treat these grafts with radiation, X-rays—everything in the spectrum. We'll grow a limb yet. We've been working on the routine tests for nearly a year now. We ought to begin the bombardment with radiation soon. Maybe then they'll be happier." He leveled the pipestem at Martin. "I won't have them quit what they're doing until they've completed it, even if I have to get a whole new staff."

Martin did not see that the doctor had scored a point, even though the doctor seemed to think he had. Can a man's employees *all* be wrong and the employer right? He felt the doctor was impressing him with certain knowledge, but information he would have given anyway. He still did not answer the question. Now, if Martin could only talk with Dr. Merrill again . . .

"If you'd care to look at these charts," the doctor said, picking them up, "you're welcome to. It may give you some idea of the vastness and completeness of the project."

"I'm afraid they wouldn't mean much to me, Dr. Penn. Actually, I'm much more interested in your personal affairs."

The doctor was amused. "Still going to do the story, eh?"

"It's a challenge, now, Dr. Penn. I still want to live with it. But one thing is bothering me."

"What's that?"

"These clothes." Martin indicated his soiled shirt, wrinkled tie, unpressed pants. "I'm afraid I'm going to have to run into Avon Ridge for my typewriter and suitcases if I'm going to stay here. I left them at the hotel." I can also make a few phone calls, he said to himself.

"You'll have a tough time doing that. Nobody gets off

the reservation for a run into town." The doctor picked up the phone. "I'll dial headquarters. Where were you staying?"

"At the Hampton. Room 317."

"You'll have them in an hour," the doctor said, his hand poised over the dial. "I'll arrange to have the bill paid and you can settle up at Inspection."

"Inspection?" There would be no phone call now; Martin was sure of that. He wondered how Forrest Killian had put in his call and whether outgoing calls from the reservation were censored.

"Everything coming in and going out is given a strict going over, Martin. Even with your credentials it wasn't easy getting in, was it?"

When he had made the arrangements, the doctor turned to him. "Inspection is about three blocks from here . . ." He paused, then pressed a buzzer. "I'd better have Virginia go with you. She knows where it is."

She came in quickly.

"Virginia," Dr. Penn said, "will you show Martin Inspection? They're bringing his stuff in from the hotel."

"They'll find the bombs in the false bottom of the suitcase," Martin said. "Maybe you'd better not be there when they open it up."

Virginia laughed. "I'll take my chances. A wet bomb can't go off. You knew they soak everything first, didn't you?"

"So we're even."

They were walking through the laboratory section when Dr. Penn called to Virginia from his office.

"Wait here, Martin. I'll be right back."

The old man is probably giving her instructions, he thought. Be sure to keep a sharp eye on Enders, he would say. Martin wondered if he would ever have a moment alone again after the previous night's violation of Penn-made rules.

He looked around him and saw a dozen men busy looking through microscopes, dissecting frogs, making marks on charts. He caught several of them eying him covertly, turning away when he returned their glances. He saw Amos Page and waved to him. He was trying to find the other two technicians he had met when he caught sight of Dr. Merrill. The head gave a signal for him to come over.

He walked nonchalantly past several men at work, approached the doctor who was remarkably clear-eyed considering how he had left him the night before.

"How are you, Doctor?"

Dr. Merrill smiled. "Couldn't be better. Ever look through a microscope?"

"In my school days," Martin admitted. "Not one of these with two eyepieces, though."

"Didn't have binocular ones when you went to school, I take it. Here, have a look."

Martin sat on the stool, put his eyes to the tubes and as he did so he felt a piece of paper being put in his hand. He was embarrassed by the action. Why couldn't the man come right out and say what he had to say? Why the mystery? Martin took a glance at something on the slide that resembled a desert strewn with driftwood. Then he got up.

"Thanks for the look," he said. "When Miss Penn comes, tell her I'll be right outside. I want some fresh air."

"The look didn't make you sick, did it?" It was Karl Gronemeier who was sitting near by. He was grinning.

"Nothing like that," Martin said, wondering if he knew about the note.

When the doors to the laboratory closed behind him he stood on the steps, lit a cigarette, opened the paper.

It read:

*If you are interested in something strange, meet me where you found me between five and six this afternoon.*

# 7

The white-haired sergeant said a truck had gone into town to fetch Martin's things. Yes, it had been dispatched about ten minutes before. No, it wouldn't be back for at least half an hour. There was nothing to do but wait and they judged by the sergeant's manner he didn't want them waiting inside.

"Tell me something," Martin said as he and Virginia left the inspection station. "Isn't anybody trusted around here?"

"What do you mean?"

"Well, I suppose I can understand why they don't want me shuttling to and from Avon Ridge, but could you or your father get off the reservation to go into town?"

"You could have," Virginia explained, "but it would have required a lot of red tape. Every time you come in or go out you've got to go through personal inspection at the gate—even after you get your pass. And then they usually want a pass application a day or two before you want to use it. The military—they're the only ones who get on and off in a hurry."

They came to a corner, turned it, walking leisurely.

"It's a funny thing," she said, glancing at him.

"What?"

"You're wanting to learn so much about Dad. Aren't we going to learn anything about you?"

"What would you like to know?"

"Well, where did you go to school?"

"I graduated from Cartwright. Is that what you wanted or do you mean the story of my life?"

She smiled prettily. She always did. It was a warm thing, her smile, and it lighted bright candles behind her eyes, the ethereal eyes that were beginning to stir him strangely.

"You might brief it down a bit."

"Well, that ought to be easy. Up to now my life has been pretty uneventful. I was born in a small town in Indiana, got interested in writing by working on the local paper. After college I served in the army three years in a tank-destroyer unit, started free lancing when I got out and was offered a job at *National Scene*. I have no family; my folks were killed in an auto crash while I was in the army. I have no brothers and sisters."

"As an only child, do you consider yourself spoiled?"

"Spoiled rotten. Hadn't you noticed?"

She laughed. "No. You keep it remarkably well hidden. What's this?"

They stopped on the sidewalk before an arbored entranceway that was clearly out of place after the severity of stone white military buildings and close-cropped grass plots. She took his arm and they walked through. Inside there were sevral benches about the lawn and bushes shut out all the reservation except the tops of the taller buildings. A rock garden, complete with a gurgling spring, took up one corner of the little park. A small sign read: Relax with Nature—Courtesy Squadron B, 23rd MP Battalion.

"How thoughtful of them," Virginia said. "I've been here a year and didn't know anything about this. Let's do as the sign says."

"Remind me to be nice to MP's from now on," Martin said as they moved to the bench nearest the small waterfall.

"I've told you my life," he said when they were seated. "Now it's your turn."

"Do you want the short form or the long form—better make it the short one. I don't think there'd be time for the full story. I've always felt close to Dad. Remember most of my life at Billingsley—he was there longest. When Mother was living it was fun and we were all happy. I even managed to get a year of college before she died and I had to take over with Bobby."

He reached for a cigarette, gave her one. As he touched a match to it, her eyes shifted to his and something smoldered behind them. He read invitation there, and it moved him. Yet he saw something else, something calculating and purposeful that made her desirable because it made her all the more unknown and challenging. The afternoon was suddenly warm. The match nearly burned his fingers before he had his own cigarette burning.

They sat in silence then, listening to the water run over the rocks, vaguely aware of the movement of motor vehicles somewhere on the reservation, the clatter of carpenters' hammers somewhere farther away.

"What do you think of Dad?" she said suddenly.

"Why do you ask that? It's too general a question."

"You haven't been getting along too well with him, have you, Martin? You shouldn't have said what you did about Bobby, you know. That upset him."

"I'm sorry. I just asked him——"

"Bobby is just a little boy. You know him now. You've seen and heard him. All he thinks about is rocket ships and space travel and the outer galaxy, not levitation and legerdemain."

Martin studied the glowing end of his cigarette. He felt her mention of the incident was a reprimand, but he did not want to argue with her about it. It also revealed that she and her father must have talked things over.

"Why didn't you go to the movie last night?"

He laughed but she did not smile. "Your father asked me that already this morning. Why is everybody so concerned about whether or not I went to the movie?"

"Dad would have told you all you wanted to know. You didn't have to ask those men about him."

Had he misinterpreted her eyes? She wasn't really angry, was she? Could this be a game?

"I didn't ask anyone about him, Virginia. They merely talked to each other and I listened. As a matter of fact, they only told me they couldn't discuss anything with me."

She looked at him now. "Do they like my father?"

"Underneath I think they do. They were just objecting to some of his methods. They——"

Now her eyes were angry. "They would object to you, too, if you were the one who told them what to do. They have a soft job, an easy berth with civil service and they are bored because security prevents their leaving the reservation. They are fed up, so they pick on their boss." She snapped her fingers. "I wouldn't give you a dime a dozen for the likes of them."

He put his cigarette out by arcing it into the water.

She followed it with her eyes, then crushed her own under her heel in the grass. "And that Dr. Merrill. He's a detriment to the whole project. He's a drunken bum. Once he was a brilliant man. I don't see how my father puts up with him."

A bell ringing somewhere in Martin's brain told him the girl lacked conviction. He wondered why she and her father—and Bobby—continued to sound off-key. He had been around enough—it was his business to analyze people and he had a special aptitude for it—yet the three Penns were baffling. There was something lacking in the fiber, something peculiar to the weave—or perhaps it was something added, something *alien*.

The incident with Bobby, the disappearance of Forrest Killian—in a test tube, Dr. Merrill said—and the strange experience of Ethel Winters, the alternate hot and cold personalities of the Penns themselves; they added up to something out of the ordinary. What was it?

He thought of the scrap of paper he had in his pocket in which Dr. Merrill had written about "something strange." He had already seen enough strange things, what he wanted now was a reason, a motive for these things. Not something new. If he could uncover the mystery he would then have something really unusual for *National Scene*. The whole affair was beginning to transcend the pretense of a mere cover story on a personality. He hoped that whatever it was, it would be something innocent so that he could use it. The thought of General Deems descending on the reservation with an army of CIC men did not end the story the way he would want it.

"What time is it?" she asked. "Hadn't we better go?"

He looked at his wrist watch. "We've got ten minutes."

She had taken his wrist to look at the watch and as she did so a blonde forelock fell over her eye. Without thinking he brushed it back and she smiled at him. "I'm afraid I sounded angry with you," she said. "I'm not, really. I think you're very nice." Her eyes were glowing, her even, white teeth bright in the sun.

"I work hard at it."

"It seems natural."

"It depends upon whom I'm with," Martin countered.

She laughed, rose and extended her hands to him. She did not move away when he got to his feet to find her looking at him fetchingly.

The first kiss was gentle and he released her only to take her again. The second kiss was not gentle.

The civilian club was deserted when he got there a few minutes after five, but it started filling up shortly thereafter with people who stopped by for a beer or two before dinner. Martin bought one and sat at the same table he had taken the night before.

It had been a profitable day in spite of its bad start. Virginia talked at length about her father, and even Ethel, when they returned to the house with his clothes and typewriter after they had passed inspection, contributed to the discussion, adding recent dates and facts when needed. Bobby, when he came home from school, went to his television.

Breaking away from Virginia for his meeting with Dr. Merrill proved simpler than he thought it would be. He mentioned he was going to the club to pick up a carton of cigarettes and he held his breath for the reaction. Virginia merely suggested he pick up several packs for her while she helped Ethel with dinner. Things were going so well, in fact, that he had misgivings about the imminent meeting and felt a vague mistrust of Dr. Merrill.

The doctor appeared within the next few minutes, looked around the room before he sat down.

"Have you been waiting long?" he asked.

"No, but I don't have much time."

"Then I'll get right to the point." Dr. Merrill shifted uncomfortably in his chair. "You've probably been bawled out for talking to me." Martin started to interrupt, but the man waved him silent. "I don't know how Dr. Penn found out about it, but he cornered me the first thing this morning. He has a faculty for doing the unsuspected."

"You probably were bawled out yourself, then, weren't you?"

"I am every day. Look," he said earnestly, "I know pretty well what Dr. Penn has said to you about the project. It wouldn't take much to convince an outsider that Dr. Penn is on the right track, but believe me when I say the rest of us know better. He has a glib way of convincing the brass what he's doing is right."

The doctor lowered his voice. "He's having us go through what is standard practice in every school and university, telling us that in our experiments with frogs we're apt to run on to something new. We're just marking time. What we ought to be doing is looking for the nerve buds that are responsible for regeneration, for it is these special nerves that innervate the structure which has to be restored and it could be the key to the metamorphosis of an ordinary cell to the regrowing type."

"That's all very interesting, but——"

"If regeneration is due to the localized persistence of embryonic tissue, or of rejuvenescent cells whose formative factors are activated by a stimulus, we ought to be looking for such a tissue in man, we ought to be seeking the stimulus responsible. Another tack might be looking into our own body cells to discover what part the cytochrome plays in our growth, how it might be used to regenerate lost parts. In insects this substance is secreted by cells acted upon by hormones and it helps some insects through their amazing metamorphosis. We haven't looked into so many things. We ought to be doing any one of them instead of cutting up frogs like high-school students."

"That," Martin said to the out-of-breath scientist, "is a matter between you and Dr. Penn. I wouldn't know which of you is right."

Dr. Merrill sat back, adjusted his glasses. "He *has* got you doubting, hasn't he? Oh, he's a smooth one, all right."

"I'm sorry," Martin said, drinking the last of his beer. "It looks like a difference of opinion to me. Is that the 'strange thing' you were going to talk to me about?"

The doctor shook his head. "No. Now I'm not sure I want to tell you about that."

"Why not?"

Dr. Merrill leaned toward him on the table. "Last night I was drunk. I don't remember what I said exactly, except that I mentioned something about Forrest Killian. Something I have never said to anyone else. Something I wouldn't dare say. Even when they had the investigation I never volunteered the information. You see, I was the last man, outside of Dr. Penn, to see Forrest Killian."

"From what you said last night," Martin said drily, "Forrest Killian walked into Dr. Penn's laboratory and never walked out again. Is that right?"

The doctor looked around, studied the nearest faces before answering.

"I saw it happen," he said guardedly. "But that *still* isn't what I mean. Look, what are you doing right after dinner?"

"Virginia and I are going to a movie," he said truthfully. She had playfully insisted he see a reservation movie and he agreed to go, though he felt he ought to talk to Dr. Penn instead.

"Isn't there some way you can get out of it?"

"I don't want to get out of it."

"It's like that, eh?"

"Can't you just tell me?"

"I don't want to do that. I want to show you."

"How long would it take?"

"I don't know. That depends upon someone else."

"Who?"

"I can't tell you that. When do you think you can get away? It has to be some night just after dinner."

Martin considered. "I don't know how long I'll be here," he parried. "Suppose you drop in here each night about this time. The night I can make it, I'll let you know. It may be tomorrow or the next day. I'll try to lay the groundwork for it."

"I'll come in here every night at this time."

"It ought to be worth while," Martin warned. "I don't want to cross the doctor again."

Dr. Merrill smiled mysteriously. "It will be worth while, don't worry," he said. "You'll wish you had come sooner." His face sobered. "You won't take me seriously until you see for yourself. It's very important that you do. You see, I find in you something I found in Forrest Killian. I liked him and he was my friend. That's why I'm talking to you like this. Anything I can do for him I want to do. You'll see."

# 8

It was only because Virginia asked him to that Martin consented to go to the area movies. He found it increasingly difficult to say no to her. It was an interesting movie, but not from the point of view of the film; he was conscious of this girl at his side all during the picture, this blonde girl with the hazy, blue eyes, this girl whose beauty was like an aura around her. Her presence fired his mind and he found himself looking at her more than the picture. When she answered the squeeze of his hand and looked at him, he could see her smile in the reflection of light from the screen and his heart hammered wildly.

The mood persisted even after he kissed her good night and he went to his room, the remembrance of it a tingling area on his lips. He could not bring himself to think of his work when there was this to remember. Her image formed before his eyes when they had closed for sleep.

*He enjoyed that because in his sleep he could do what he wished with her. He suggested that she wear a negligee and there she was in it, floating just off the bed.*

*"Do you prefer me like this?" she asked sweetly.*

*"I like you any way," he said. "You're wonderful."*

*"You've been thinking that all evening," she said, blushing. "You're apt to turn my head."*

*He sat up and she waved him down.*

*"You're supposed to be getting your rest," she said. "Now why don't you just lie there and tell me your troubles?"*

*"I don't have any troubles when you're around."*

*"You might have troubles tomorrow," she said, smiling coquettishly.*

*"What kind of troubles will they be?"*

*"Oh, you'll start thinking you're spending too much time with me." She pouted. "Would you really think that?"*

*"No!" he almost shouted.*

*"Not so loud," she laughed. "Now, do you promise you won't think that?"*

*"Yes. I swear it."*

*"If you do think about it, you must remember the way to learn about a man is to live with his family, much as you*

*are doing with us. You mustn't think of anything else, understand?"*

*He nodded. "I understand."*

*"Ethel may be a bit curious about us," she said. "But you won't let that bother you, will you? Ethel just doesn't understand how we feel about each other, does she?"*

*"No. Ethel doesn't."*

*The smile was beautiful. "I like you more and more." The gentle breeze rippled the negligee and revealed the girl's charms in the shadowless light of the room.*

*"I love you," he said ardently.*

*"I know, darling. And another thing. You've been seeing too much of that Dr. Merrill, don't you think? Dad is going to get angry if you don't confine your attention to him. After all, this story you're doing is supposed to be about Dad, remember?"*

*"Of course. I'm sorry, Virginia."*

*"Dr. Merrill is against Dad. Dr. Merrill wants to hurt Dad. I don't like Dr. Merrill, do you?"*

*"No. I don't like Dr. Merrill."*

*"Something ought to happen to him, don't you think?"*

*"Yes, something ought to happen to Dr. Merrill."*

*Virginia smoothed the negligee and Martin followed the hands with an avid gaze.*

*"We can talk about that later. Perhaps in a day or two, Martin."*

*"Anything you say, Virginia."*

*"I think you're swell, Martin. Dad does, too. You'll find his attitude changed. He'll probably think we're in love. Maybe he's right. . . ."*

When Martin awakened it was not the rude awakening from total sleep but the exchanging of a mellow, friendly dream state for the more exciting reality of his imminent nearness to Virginia, for he remembered he had a dream in which she figured prominently.

During the next three days the glow he felt in her presence ripened to a fierce fire and he was with her constantly. After all, he reasoned when he felt he might be spending too much time with her, the way to learn about a man is to live with his family. He didn't care because Ethel seemed to disapprove, looking at him searchingly and sometimes disdainfully. Ethel probably had never felt the way he did. He didn't mind that Dr. Penn smiled when he walked in on them talking softly and earnestly in the living room, her lips an inch from his; the smile amounted to paternal consent, didn't it? And he was supposed to get on the good side of the man, wasn't he? How else could he ever learn anything? He could always talk to Dr. Penn later.

It was on the third day at the laboratory that he came face to face with Dr. Merrill in the washroom.

"Hi," Martin said, nodding in recognition on his way out.

The doctor, who was entering, grabbed his arm and pulled him around. The door hissed shut behind him.

"For God's sake, what's happened to you? You're following that girl around like a puppy."

Anger flared deep in Martin's mind. Here was a man who was standing in Dr. Penn's way—good Dr. Penn. He suddenly hated Dr. Merrill and his arm flashed upward to strike him. The doctor's forearm caught the blow and the momentary pain was like a hot wire running to his brain.

Martin's well-being evaporated. Cold sweat began to ooze through his pores with the realization that he had almost hit the doctor and he stood there, chilled and chagrined at what he had done. The pain cleared his head.

"I'm—I'm sorry, Dr. Merrill," he said, confused.

The doctor, who had been standing there in wonder, dropped his arm slowly. "I had no idea it was like that," he said quietly.

"Believe me, I can't understand what possessed me to do a thing like that, Doctor."

"You are not to blame," the doctor said. "Now I know why you didn't come each night."

Martin's face flushed. He had not given a thought to the rendezvous with Dr. Merrill and this knowledge washed over him with new wonderment. How could he have forgotten that he was to meet the doctor at the civilian club when he could get away? It didn't make sense.

"I guess I've been too busy," Martin said miserably.

The doctor shook his head but kept his eyes on Martin. "No, that isn't the reason. The same thing happened to Forrest Killian, Martin. He was the most inquisitive man, the most friendly guy the first few weeks I knew him. Then something happened to him and he did not spend his nights in the barracks any longer and when I saw him during the day he was unfriendly and cold. Suddenly he seemed to snap out of it and he confessed to me he had been as one possessed and then . . . I can't tell you about that now."

"Was it—was it the girl?"

"It was the girl. He never told me where he was when he wasn't in his room at night, but I have a good idea. He told me he had dreams."

The shock of it stiffened Martin and something cold settled

around his heart. Had she been as friendly as that with Forrest Killian? Had she entered Forrest's dreams as she had entered his? Was he treading the same path as the unfortunate laboratory technician, the path that ended—where?

With effort now he recalled that General Deems had said Forrest called him after two weeks to tell him he didn't suspect anyone. Virginia must have been controlling him then much as she had evidently controlled Martin for the past three days. Then, as the general had told, the agent called one night to say he had found what he was looking for and that he suspected Dr. Penn and would call the general after he had confronted the doctor with the evidence.

*What manner of girl was this?* He ruled out hypnosis in favor of something much more forceful. He could understand now Forrest's sudden awakening and his setting himself against what he knew of them and arming himself with the evidence and confronting the doctor with it. That was the end of Forrest Killian, presumably.

"The same thing happened to me one night," Dr. Merrill was saying. "Only I would always wake up. I got drunk the first time I spouted off against the doctor. So he and Virginia took me to their home. I passed out and the next thing I knew I was having a dream and both of them were there asking me questions. But I would wake up each time, only to pass out again and there they'd be shooting those questions at me. I finally sobered enough to walk out of the house. A patrolling military police squad took me home. Nearly lost my job because of it. If it weren't for the fact I've got influence in Washington, I think I would have been kicked out, for I understand Dr. Penn tried his best to get rid of me."

For a moment Dr. Merrill was lost in amused reminiscence, then he sighed, returned to the present and, with a look at Martin, said, "I wouldn't take it so hard, Martin. I never did see any overt action on her part toward Forrest, if that's what's worrying you; she was always cool toward him around the laboratory. At least with you she seems to be putting her heart in it."

Martin snorted. "Maybe I'm just a little harder to convince than Forrest. I want you to know I'm familiar with this dream technique and because you mentioned it a lot of things are beginning to clear up for me. Will you be at the civilian club after dinner?"

"If you're still interested."

"I'm very interested. What time should I be there?"

"You must be there by six thirty. Any later than that and you needn't come at all."

"I'll be there. I don't know how I'm going to make it,

but I will. Dinner at the Penns' isn't over until around seven, you know."

"I know. That's why I want you there at six thirty."

Martin fixed him with a questioning stare. The doctor merely answered with a quizzical smile.

"I'll see you at six thirty, then," Martin said, turning determinedly on his heel and leaving the room.

"I hope you make it."

For the rest of the afternoon Martin tried to put the zest he knew he should have felt in his work with Virginia in the office of Dr. Penn, comparing charts and reading figures and occasionally lapsing into an episode in each other's lives. But he knew it was not convincing. His mind went back to what Dr. Merrill had to say and back to the point in the washroom when he had suddenly realized he had been as one hypnotized.

The girl did not seem capable of it. Virginia was laughing and gay and she bubbled with good humor and amusing anecdotes. Only once in a while did she give any evidence of being anything else when he caught her looking at him furtively. Even then, when he caught her at it, she turned into something pretty, flashing him that contagious smile and asking him what he was looking at. He found it impossible not to humor her.

But she knew. She knew because when he told her at five o'clock, the usual time they started for home, that he did not feel well and was going to go to his room and would not come down later for dinner, she gave him a long and searching look.

"You've changed suddenly," she said. "Something's happened."

They were walking along a hedge-lined street and she kept slightly ahead of him, looking back at him.

"You've not been yourself this afternoon, darling. What's the matter?" she asked questioningly, solicitously.

"It's just as I said. I don't feel well. That's all." He wished she wouldn't question him.

"But one just doesn't *feel* well. There's something he doesn't feel well *about*. What is it? Your stomach? Do you have a headache? Or isn't it physical?" There was an accent on the latter.

"Do I have to give a list of symptoms? I just don't feel well all over. Call it what you will. Besides, I have no appetite and I want to think. Is there anything wrong in wanting to think?"

Virginia let him catch up and walked by his side, silent for a few steps. Then, "Is it something I've done?"

"No."

"Then at least you know that it isn't anything I've done. At least that much is definite. Now, is it something Dad's done?"

He stopped and she stopped. They faced each other.

"Look," he said patiently. "This will get us no place. You're being just like a woman. Can't you tell when a man wants to be alone, to think things out? It only makes me feel worse to have you bombarding me with questions."

In the end she walked by his side silently, meekly, and said nothing when they entered the house. He went up to his room and lay on the bed.

It was 5:15. He had more than an hour.

The late afternoon sun streamed through the windows and the curtains, fluttering in the breeze, were a symphony of movement, their shadows on the wallpaper. This time of the afternoon was always unreal, he reflected, the sun being so low in the heavens, there being such long shadows and that something in the atmosphere that let only the red rays come through, bathing everything in a ruddy glow. That curtain, for example, and that color and the moving, changing pattern. Why, it changed a million times and it could be anything—even a face . . .

*The face of Virginia, for example.*

*"Martin," Virginia said sweetly from the curtain.*

*He struggled hard against the pleasant, soothing sensation emanating from the face and he looked away and suddenly an abyss opened beneath him and he plummeted down, his last glimpse of the face showing Virginia's puzzlement and concern.*

He awoke, startled.

The late afternoon sun streamed through the windows and the curtains, fluttering in the breeze, were a symphony of movement, their shadows on the wallpaper. That curtain, the color and movement, *it could be a face . . .*

He forced himself to sit up before the face said anything and it was gone. He put the knuckle of his forefinger in his mouth and bit down on it hard. He felt his breath on his hand as he did so. He was sleepy, sleepier than he had ever been before and he wanted so much to lie down.

It was 5:25. He had more than an hour.

The late afternoon sun . . .

He got to his feet and moved around the room. He took out a cigarette and found that his hand shook as he lit it. He went to the window and stood there. All was quiet in the street. Everybody was in his house waiting for dinner. There was only the well-kept grass, the long shadows of the sun, the gentle movement of the curtains past his cheeks.

*And the girl out there moving along the street. Martin wondered vaguely where she lived. She had a walk that he knew, a graceful, feminine walk, and it did not seem unusual that she should suddenly walk to the second-floor window from out in the street. It was Virginia. What an odd way to come to see him!*

*He grinned. Virginia was full of tricks.*

*Virginia's face was just on the other side of the window now.*

*"Martin," she said sweetly. "Let me help you, won't you?"*

*A dull ache ran from his fingers to his shoulders and to his brain. The ache became a pain and the pain became unbearable.*

Martin's cigarette was burning his hand. He saw its smoldering head just a moment before he dashed it to the floor and saw the ashes splatter over the rug. He ran about stamping on the glowing ashes.

His shirt was sticking to his back. Sweat that had collected on his forehead trickled down beside his eyes. He wet his lips with a dry tongue, tasted sweat.

There was a gentle movement of the curtains at the window.

With a cry he went to the door, flung it open and started down the stairs. At the bottom he came upon Dr. Penn who stared at him. For a moment Martin hesitated, then he rushed past out the front door.

He saw Virginia sitting on the steps. He hesitated again, then ran down the steps past her.

"Martin!"

He turned.

"Wait!"

Virginia ran up to him.

"Get away from me!" he yelled, backing away toward the street.

"No, Martin!" She came up to him, reached for him, but he eluded her hands.

"Haven't you done enough? What are you?"

Martin was shocked to see tears rimming her eyes, to find her shoulders slumped as she brought her hands up to her face to cover it.

"If you could only understand!" Virginia implored.

"What's there to understand?" He stood there on the parkway, practically shouting, wary lest she get too near.

"Oh, Martin!" She was racked by sobs.

"For God's sake!"

"You needn't shout so the whole neighborhood can hear!"

"Hear what? It seems to me you are the one who should be shouting, trying to explain."

"I know. You just don't understand. You never will. Something's happened and you think you know something. I was only trying to warn you, if what I think is true. Even Dad wasn't aware of it." Virginia glanced back at the house but no one was in sight. She dried her eyes.

"Martin, you have come to mean a lot to me. You know that, don't you?"

"Is that why you tried to reach me just a little while ago, tried to get me asleep so you could talk some sense into me again?"

"Oh!" She put her hand over her mouth in horror. "Even to know *that* much. Martin, what are you going to do?"

He laughed derisively. "Virginia, what kind of a fool do you take me for, a complete one?"

"You think you know something!"

"So?"

She reached up and before he could move away she had the ends of his shirt collar in her hands.

"Martin, even a little knowledge is bad. Why were you ever assigned here!"

"Sometimes I wonder."

"It started off wrong, I should have known. If you hadn't seen Bobby . . ."

He tensed. This was something new. "Bobby?"

She nodded. "You wouldn't be living with us—Oh, I can't tell you!" Virginia was agitated and pulled at his collar. "Why don't you get out of here before it's too late! Go to the dispensary and tell them something—anything to get you off the reservation."

He put his hands on his hips and looked at her disdainfully. "Why? Would you mind telling me that?"

"Nothing good can come of what you think you know." She tugged harder at the collar now, her eyes round and concerned. "Get out of the reservation while you can. I was trying to tell you that—back there—trying to make you get out, but you wouldn't let me and I could see that you were going to do something——"

"Something," he said. "You mean something like what Forrest Killian did. Is that it?"

Her hands dropped from the collar. Her mouth went slack and for a moment she looked tired and bewildered and frightened.

"I know about you and Forrest, how you led him around —until the end."

She did not move.

He turned and walked down the street, expecting her to follow him and possibly explain. But his own feet were the only ones he heard in the dusk. Half a block down he looked back.

She was still standing there in the growing shadows, a lonely figure looking after him, making no sign that she saw him.

He went on.

# 9

Now he was in trouble. He had alienated Virginia and probably her father. Yet what else could he have done? Let her dominate him again as she had for three days? What manner of woman was she to be able to do this and to appear as she had in his room? It was beyond anything he had ever heard of or read.

Then there was her hint about Bobby, implying that because of what he had seen Bobby do, he was staying at the Penn house. Why? And did she mean to admit that Bobby had actually performed those strange things he had seen the boy do? If that was true, then this was more than fantastic—it was unbelievable. But then, magician's tricks look impossible. Then when it is explained . . . Perhaps there was an explanation for this.

He thought of it as a magazine story and this made him think of *National Scene* and thinking of the magazine with its calm, solidly factual reporting of the most complex but material things of this world filled him with a longing to be back in the office. Perhaps if he could think this thing out in a familiar place faraway from Park Hill he might be able to reach a conclusion that would resolve the problem.

But I'm not at *National Scene*. I'm right here at Park Hill where this thing is happening and I'm working both for the magazine and for General Deems. He grimaced when he thought of the general. If I call him about this right now, he'll think I've lost my mind. I've got to get to the bottom of it first. I've got to understand it myself before I start talking to anyone else about it.

As he walked along the street to the civilian club, he planned his moves. He would not return to the Penn house. He would be putting himself in Virginia's hands again if he did that. He felt sure the dream power of whatever it was that the girl had could not reach him if he stayed with Dr. Merrill for the night. Then the next morning he would take the matter to Colonel Sherrington. The commanding officer of the reservation ought to be willing to work with him on it. If the name *National Scene* was not enough, then Martin could tell the colonel about General Deems. Then there would be action. Martin almost grinned at the thought of what the mention of the CIC would mean in the office of Colonel Sherrington.

He felt satisfied the way he had things figured out, walked into the civilian club with a brisk step and a smile on his face. He almost laughed when he saw the serious face of Dr. Merrill, it looked so woebegone.

Dr. Merrill half rose from his seat, shook hands solemnly and then sat down with Martin.

"I've been sitting here worrying about you," the doctor said. "But I needn't have. It's only six o'clock. How did you get away?"

"I almost didn't," Martin said. He recounted his dream experience with Virginia.

"I've felt that was happening all along," Dr. Merrill said. "That's what I meant when I seemed surprised that you would be staying at Dr. Penn's house. They tried that dream stuff on me, you remember. For some reason it didn't take. Or maybe they didn't try hard enough. They really had no reason to try it with me. I had been only too talkative against Dr. Penn." Then he added, as an afterthought, "You can't go back there, naturally."

"I'd like to stay with you tonight, if you don't mind."

"There are a lot of rooms vacant in P-4. The one next to mine, for example. But that can come later. We'd better be on our way."

"If it's any of my business, where are we going?"

Dr. Merrill smiled mysteriously again. "To the laboratory. Come on."

"For all of the urgency regarding Penn Project," Dr. Merrill said as he inserted his key into the lock, "there is no night work. For that we can be thankful."

He opened the door and they went inside. The place was deserted. The door clicked shut behind them and they stood there, listening. The only sounds were usual ones from the reservation outside, others were the drip of a faucet, a barely audible hum of a motor somewhere in the building and sounds from some of the animal cages.

The dusk had so deepened by this time lights from the street were beginning to illuminate the opaque windows at the far end of the building in the laboratory working area.

"We'll stay in my office here," Dr. Merrill said, walking into it. "I never lock the door like the others. Too much bother."

The doctor carried two stools to a place behind the door. "We'll sit on these," he said. "We'll be behind this door. So." He sat on a stool and motioned for Martin to do the same. When Martin had sat down, he said, "From where you sit now you ought to be able to see the reflection of Dr. Penn's office door in the window there behind my desk. We will see this little drama from here, always looking in the window."

"What are we going to see?"

The doctor got down from the stool, took off his coat and laid it on a near-by table. Martin did the same.

"I'd prefer not to tell you," the doctor said. "It might not occur; then you wouldn't believe me. No, this way is better."

They sat on the stools in silence for a while. Then Dr. Merrill spoke again.

"I can say this, though. One afternoon right after work I went to the civilian club and had a bottle with me. I was pretty disgusted with the way things were going here at the lab that day—oh, it was in May, I guess. Well, I thought it would be a wonderful night to forget it all, so I took a drink out of the bottle and then had a beer. I continued with these boilermakers for quite a while.

"I hadn't eaten anything, so the stuff really went to my head after about six of them. I didn't want to go back to the barracks because I didn't think I'd make it up the stairs. Besides, I thought I might get sick, which is unusual for me, for I don't get sick very often any more.

"I came here and sat in the office with the lights off trying to sober up. I saw the whole thing and it sobered me plenty. I came back the next night to see if it was true and I've been coming back quite often, but I've never been able to figure it out—you'll see what I mean."

"All right, if you say so," Martin said. "I still would like to know what to expect."

"Be patient. You'll see." The doctor got off the stool and adjusted the door for the best opening. Then he looked at his watch. "It's after six thirty," he said, coming back to the stool. "It ought to be any minute now."

Martin ground his teeth in impatience. What was Dr. Merrill trying to prove? Why didn't he just explain? If this thing involved Virginia or Dr. Penn, then perhaps Martin would be seeing either of them again and he didn't want to—at this time. There would be plenty of time after he saw Colonel Sherrington.

"I can't understand this dream business," Dr. Merrill said softly beside him. "That is a real puzzler. Where do you suppose they learned how to do that? Something like Yogi or mind power or something similar to what you see advertised in the magazines."

Martin thought about telling him what he saw Bobby do, decided this was neither the time nor place to start.

"There's bound to be a logical explanation for it," the doctor went on. "Everything has an explanation. Take a magician. He cuts off a woman's head. That's what it looks as if he were doing, but he's not, of course. Or sawing a woman in half. Our eyes are easily fooled. Perhaps our minds are fooled as readily. There's a scientific explanation for it. There must be."

Martin was not in the mood to discuss it.

Suddenly there was a sound and Dr. Merrill caught his arm. They were still and silent.

The lock was turning, there was a step into the laboratory. The door swung open almost noiselessly. Then it clicked shut behind someone. Whoever it was stood silent for a while and Martin hoped his breathing, which was audible to him, did not carry out into the corridor.

There was a click of a switch and the corridor blazed into light. Martin unconsciously slumped his shoulders and made himself as small as possible. The doctor's hand on his arm steadied him. It was so bright in the corridor they surely would be seen on their stools in the window.

Dr. Penn moved into the rectangle of light Martin could see reflected in the white window. He did not look into the room. He brought out a key, inserted it in his office door lock, turned it, opened the door and went in to turn on a light. He came out, went down the hall and turned out the light there before returning to his office and closing the door.

"The door!" Martin breathed in dismay. "He's closed it!"

"That's all right," Dr. Merrill whispered.

Martin failed to see how anything could happen before their eyes if the door was closed. From where he sat he could see a ribbon of bright light under the door and every now and then Dr. Penn's shadow blotted out part of it.

For a long time there was no activity in the office and Martin's spine wearied, sitting on the stool. What could it be, this senseless sitting on stools watching a door?

After a wait of several more minutes there was an odd sensation in the air. It was as if a cold breeze had suddenly blown in from somewhere. With a quickening heart Martin remembered a similar sensation when he watched a small boy with a sphere.

"I think it's about time," Dr. Merrill said, relaxing.

"He'll hear you," Martin warned.

Dr. Merrill laughed in his normal voice and Martin felt like hitting him. Why did the man invite discovery?

"I don't think so," Dr. Merrill said. "You'll see. Just follow me." The doctor got off the stool and the sounds seemed thunderous compared to the preceding quiet. He went to the door to Dr. Penn's office and, selecting a key from his ring, inserted it in the lock. "I had this key especially made for this," he said.

Martin's heart was beating fast. Was the man mad? What possible reason could they give for entering Dr. Penn's office?

Dr. Merrill swung the door open and they both entered the office.

It was empty.

Dr. Merrill watched Martin's eyes dart around seeking out all the possible hiding places.

"See what luck *you* have, Martin," Dr. Merrill said. "I've tapped every board and every square inch of this room. There must be an exit somewhere. He must have opened something and gone out. But what? And *why?*"

This was a page from when knighthood was in flower, when there were secret panels in the castles for escape in case of danger, but surely not in this age and on a military reservation!

"Looking for someone?"

They whirled around to the voice at the door.

Dr. Penn stood there, smiling. He entered the room and closed the door behind him. He did not move from it.

"This is unfortunate," he said. The way he said it made Martin's blood run to his feet, leaving him dizzy. There was something about this man he had not noticed before, a magnetic quality, a hazy look about the eyes. He had not noticed before how much like Virginia's eyes they were.

"If you will sit down, please." Dr. Penn motioned to a laboratory stool and his desk chair. "I don't know how to tell you this, but you present quite a problem. Both of you. If you disappear there are sure to be repercussions. The question is: What am I going to do with you? You can't go back knowing what you know."

"What do we know?" Dr. Merrill managed to ask.

"It isn't exactly what you know," the doctor said in a calm, controlled voice. "It's what the recitation of your experiences here might imply. That we could not allow."

"Who is 'we'?" Martin asked.

The doctor showed his yellowed teeth in a wide grin. "You *have* been curious, haven't you, Martin? I can see what my daughter sees in you, all right. I witnessed your little argument with her tonight. It must be unsettling to be confronted with something you cannot be expected to understand, Martin."

Where were you? Martin wanted to ask him. I didn't see you when I looked back.

"As long as you're in such a talkative mood, Dr. Penn," Dr. Merrill said, "why not tell us why you are standing in the way of regeneration?"

From somewhere the doctor produced one of his Missouri meerschaums. Martin could have sworn he was nowhere near a pipe a moment before. He struck a match and sucked on the pipe slowly and methodically.

"You won't believe me, Dr. Merrill," Dr. Penn said, "when I tell you I hated like the devil running that project in the wrong direction. You sensed that. It was a point in your favor that you did. The fact that you objected, that you were disgusted with me, was a fine display of the real scientific spirit, the kind of spirit your world needs and needs desperately. But at the moment regeneration cannot be. You are not ready for it yet."

"Not ready for it!" Dr. Merrill's eyes grew fiery and veins in his forehead enlarged. "Who do you think you are to judge whether or not regeneration ought to be? Let me tell you something. It's because of the brass hats you're fooling in Washington——"

"Who's talking about brass hats? You influenced several to keep you here when I wanted to get rid of you," Dr. Penn said archly. "What about that?" The doctor shook his head. "You would have earned more respect if you had left of your own accord. Instead, you allowed that incident and the geometrical progression of incidents in your mind to lead you to drink, an escapist's way out. What did it get you? This. Believe me when I say it is without rancor that I tell you this: You mean nothing to me one way or another."

"Talk, talk, talk!" Dr. Merrill was white with anger. "You talk about the scientific spirit! Ha! Your brain isn't big enough to contain a cubic millimeter of spirit, scientific or otherwise!"

Dr. Penn was amused and showed it. "Tut, tut," he said, aggravating the man still further. "You're exhibiting the size of your brain right now."

"What about *National Scene?*" Martin said. "Your admission that you are preventing regeneration research certainly won't look good."

Dr. Penn looked at him gravely. "You still do not understand. There will be no *National Scene* story as surely as there will be no *you*. As I've said, this is a problem for which I have no immediate solution—the problem of how to dispose of you two gentlemen. It will have dangerous consequences regardless of how it is accomplished."

"I always thought you were off your trolley," Dr. Merrill said, getting off his stool. "Now I know it." He started for the door.

"Where do you think you're going?" Dr. Penn asked, stepping aside.

"I'm going straight to Colonel Sherrington. I should have done it long ago."

Dr. Merrill opened the door, started to walk through the doorway, but collided with a black wall and fell back into the room.

"There is no way out of this room at the moment," Dr. Penn said. "There won't be until I have solved this problem."

"The whole room is an elevator then, is that it?" Dr. Merrill snarled. "Well, you can take us back up again."

"Perceptually, not bad. Conceptually, very poor, Dr. Merrill. Oh, don't stand there like a damned fool. Don't you suppose I've known about you? I've been thinking all evening about what I should do. You see, I knew you were behind the door to your office the first night and each night you've been here since. But I didn't care. It wasn't important as long as you never did anything about it. When we examined your drunken mind that night at my home while you slept we discovered you knew nothing about us. If you had, you wouldn't be here now."

Martin, who had been listening and watching Dr. Penn, saw his expression change ever so slightly. There was the merest flicker of an eyelid, a more intent look about the eyes. Martin looked at Dr. Merrill to see what had caused the change.

Dr. Merrill had a gun in his hand. Martin could see the lettering on its side: COLT CAL .45. He wondered where he got it, but a man who can get whisky on a military reservation ought not have too much trouble filching a service automatic . . .

"Now, Dr. Penn," Dr. Merrill said in a voice strained with tension. "The funny stuff is over. We're through listening to your lecture. Now we want to listen to a few of your answers."

"Take it easy, Doctor," Martin said.

"I don't know where you got that, Dr. Merrill," Dr. Penn said, unperturbed. "I suggest you put it away and forget you ever brought it out."

"Think I'm a fool?"

Martin did not like the tone of Dr. Merrill's voice. He did not like the look in his eyes. They were wide and round and his face was blanched, his lips a grim, white line. Sweat stood out on his forehead.

"I'm giving you a warning," Dr. Penn said levelly, never moving from his spot beside the open door.

"Are you going to talk?" The words were like whiplashes, but they fell on unyielding substance, for the doctor never moved.

The release of the safety catch was like the snapping of a giant spring and the sound jarred the three men in the room.

They all stood as if in tableau, the doctor by the door, looking hard at the man with the gun, Dr. Merrill leaning forward, his finger circling the trigger determinedly, Martin still sitting in Dr. Penn's chair, undecided what he should do.

Dr. Penn vanished.

All that remained was a curling wisp of pipe smoke that dissolved in the air. There was a feeling that somewhere a door had blown open.

Dr. Merrill and Martin stared, unbelieving. Dr. Merrill stood as if sculptured, leaning slightly forward, tense, taut and rigid, eyes on the spot where Dr. Penn had stood.

Suddenly there was a frenzy of motion and Dr. Merrill was gone, gun and all.

Then there was more motion, a blinding flash.

All thought and life for Martin Enders had ceased.

# 10

In the infinite blackness of space there was nothing. No star shone. He was part of it, this absence of matter, of light, of not the least suggestion of a thing material, a minus quantity native to the vacuum. He was there for an eon; he might have been there from the beginning of time, if time had begun.

From the limitless distances surrounding him there came suddenly a surge of power, seeking him out, a stream of force from the far reaches inhibited by no opposing thing, searching and finding the infinitely small parcels of his being, encompassing them. Then he understood. He had being! The shreds of life shattered and strewn beyond existence were being compressed, pushed together.

A tiny spark of light, a pin point of life like a burning candle seen across the miles on a lonely, black night appeared at the furthermost reaches of time and grew until he could see the universe before him.

Then the universe exploded and he was further pressed and diminished while nebulae, star clusters and systems raced him by. He was stronger, had form and shape now, an existence molded by the force drawing him like a magnet. The final blaze of blurring, rushing stars flashed outward and then there was peace. He was whole again.

"Martin!"

With effort, he opened his eyes. A girl stood before him. Virginia's face was gaunt, her eyes concerned. Her lips moved.

"Can you hear me?" The sound of the words came afterward, as when a sound film is not synchronized. It was peculiar.

"Yes." It was all he could do to reply.

"Martin, do not try to do anything just yet. Listen to me. You were gone. I almost couldn't bring you back, you had gone so far."

"Gone?" He did not understand.

"Yes. You were destroyed . . . Oh, no matter, darling. Listen: You are in danger. *We* are in danger."

"We are?"

"Martin!" she cried in frenzy. She slapped at his face. He hardly felt the sting of her hands.

"For God's sake, Martin!" She looked around in anguish. Then she came close to him, her hazy blue eyes only a few inches from his. "Think, Martin! Think!"

Suddenly the haze was gone and he was shocked by the clarity of his own vision. He could see her eyes clearly now, for the first time. He could see *through* them . . .

Then he knew. In a moment he saw what had happened, why her voice was filled with urgency.

"I—I was *dead?*"

"Yes, darling. You didn't—exist any more."

"And you brought me back."

She smiled through tears. "Yes."

"And—and Dr. Merrill . . . ?"

He saw in her eyes the vastness of the outer reaches where he had gone.

"Your father. He did this?"

"Yes." Tears flowed. "I pleaded with him. He told me I could not have you, that I couldn't bring you back. I betrayed him for you. We mustn't stay here."

She got up but he did not move.

Suddenly she was shaking him. Then she grasped his hands, tried pulling him to his feet. "Get up, Martin!" she urged.

He tried moving his limbs, felt the blood flow in them as if for the first time. If he had been dead . . . He noticed they were still in Dr Penn's office.

"Dr. Penn?" he asked.

"He's not here now, praise God," she said. "He thinks you are gone—like Dr. Merrill. That's why we've got to get you out of here before he comes back."

"He disappeared."

She nodded. "He went—" She smiled. "Never mind."

The air outside felt good as it brushed Martin's cheeks. He continued to hold the girl's hand as they walked along the sidewalk; there was strength in her and it flowed to him when he touched her. He needed that strength, for he was still unable to move fast or think clearly.

"Where are we going?" he asked.

"We've got to go to the house," she said.

"Why?"

"There is no time to explain."

The air and the brisk walk along the street were reviving him. While he was still dazed, he felt safer following her than he would have felt left at the laboratory. The girl had rescued him. Otherwise he would be what Forrest Killian and Dr. Merrill no doubt were: nonexistent. Therefore, he'd better mind what she said. Or was this all a dream she was creating in his mind? The thought made him dizzy. A box within a box within a box within a box . . .

If she said he was in danger, it was true. Hadn't he seen it in her eyes? He did not understand the forces opposing him, so it would be wiser to put his trust in a member of the enemy who seemed to want to help him. He could not hope to combat them after what he had seen in Dr. Penn's office. If the girl was right, he would be lucky to escape with his life—his new life.

She stopped in front of the house, faced him. "Act natural if you can," she said. "Stay close to me. There is an envelope around you. It is stronger the closer you are to me."

"Good evening, Virginia, Mr. Enders," Ethel said when they passed her by in the living room. "You sure went out of here fast before, Mr. Enders. Was anything wrong?"

Virginia was going up the stairs.

"Nothing, Ethel," he said, hurrying upstairs after her. "I just remembered an appointment. I was trying to make it on time."

"Oh." Ethel was unconvinced. Martin did not think she could be one of the enemy.

Virginia went to the phone in the hallway on the second floor. "This will be away from prying ears," she explained softly.

She dialed a number.

"Send an ambulance to P-110 right away. It's an emergency. This is Virginia Penn. . . . Yes. . . . There's not time to explain. Hurry."

"What . . . ?" he started to say.

"You're sick," she said. "You've got acute appendicitis. You're all doubled up when they get here, understand?"

"Yes, but——"

"What's up, Sis?" It was Bobby coming out of his room into the hallway, his boyish eyes twinkling, his face and hands dirty.

His appearance changed unexpectedly. The eyes grew brighter with intelligence and the boy looked at Martin in wonder.

"I can feel it from here," Bobby said. "What are you trying to do, Virginia?" It was adult talk but it was a child's voice.

"Please, Robert! Try to understand."

"Where is Dad?"

"Back there."

"He came back, though. I felt two shocks. Who were they and why was it necessary?"

"You know as well as I why they were necessary."

Bobby smiled craftily. "Just who were they?"

"Dr. Merrill and——"

"And *him.*" Bobby sneered. "I felt you bring him back. Dad probably did, too. What do you think you're doing now? You did not answer before!"

"How's *Tornado Bill?*" Martin could not restrain himself, the change in the boy was so ludicrous.

Bobby shot him a scornful look. "You know the penalty, Virginia."

"I've lived many years more than you, Robert. I'm as aware as you are of the penalties involved."

"You're a fool! Protecting him in an envelope! When father gets back he'll talk sense into you."

"We're leaving, Robert."

*"They'll* find you."

"They must let him live!"

"Are you out of your mind?"

"Will you stop me?"

Bobby looked at the floor. "No," he said resignedly. "I won't stop you. Good luck."

"You won't tell Dad?"

"I won't go back for him, if that's what you mean."

"Thanks, Robert."

The boy turned and went back into his room.

"Come on," Virginia said, grasping Martin's hand and pulling him to the stairs.

The front-door chime jarred them into motion on the stairs, Martin clattering down behind the racing Virginia. Ethel was already at the door and, as she opened it, Martin collapsed at the bottom of the stairs, clutching his stomach.

A sergeant removed his hat as he stepped through the doorway. Ethel stared at the fallen figure. "What's the matter with Mr. Enders?" she asked in surprise.

"Are you alone?" Virginia asked the soldier.

"No. I got a buddy in the meat wagon outside," he said, studying Martin, who lay on the floor, groaning and lashing about. "What's the trouble with him?"

"Appendix," Virginia said. "Better get him to the hospital in a hurry. It may have burst. I'll help you."

Together, with Martin supported between them and barely able to walk, they half carried him out of the house to the ambulance. The driver jumped and opened the rear door. Then he helped them put Martin on a stretcher inside.

The truck drew away from the curb, gathered speed down the street, the two army men in front, Virginia at Martin's side in the rear.

"I can't stand it!" Martin cried in mock agony, thrashing about, hands on his stomach, teeth bared and grinding as if in pain.

"There, there, darling," Virginia comforted, stroking his forehead. "It will be all right soon."

"Oh, what's going to happen next?" he groaned, fixing her with one eye, the other closed.

"Quiet," she replied, giving him a sharp look.

"How's he making it?" the sergeant asked, turning around.

"Not too good," Virginia said.

The ambulance slowed, turned a corner. Martin, who had been watching Virginia, saw her tense, narrow her eyes and assume the manner of one in extreme concentration.

Suddenly the ambulance screeched to a lurching stop.

"I'll be damned!" the driver said, leaning forward on the wheel, staring ahead. "Where did that wall come from? It wasn't there a second ago!"

"What *is* this?" the sergeant asked no one in particular, leaning forward in order to see how high the wall was.

Martin turned his head and, through what he could see of the windshield, saw the even bricks of the wall.

The sergeant opened the car door, looked to the rear. "Hey! Can you beat that! There's a wall behind us, too!"

"What's the trouble, Sergeant?" Virginia asked concernedly. "Is this the hospital?"

"No, ma'am," he said. "It's—I don't know how to explain it. Just a minute."

Both army men got out to inspect the wall, leaving the ambulance motor running.

"Can you drive?" Virginia asked Martin.

"Sure, but——"

"Get there and drive, then," she snapped, indicating the driver's seat.

Martin clambered over the rear of the seat, gestured to the wall in front of them which ran to the houses on either side of the street. "How . . . ?"

Suddenly the wall was gone and the street stretched on in front of them.

"Let's go!" Virginia yelled.

Martin put the truck in gear and they whizzed past the two soldiers who had been examining the wall and who stood now staring at where it had been.

"Head for the gate," the girl shouted above the din of the motor. "It's straight on down this street."

"How can we get through it?" he returned.

"I don't know. There will be a way."

"Maybe those ambulance men will phone the gate."

"Maybe."

The gate was before them. It would be suicide to try to race past the lighted office and the brightly illuminated area around it. Martin slowed the ambulance, brought it to a stop as a soldier with a white helmet, sidearm and bobby stick in his belt stepped out of the building in the center of the road. Beyond was freedom.

"Your pass?" the soldier, a corporal, asked. Then he gave a start as he saw they weren't in uniform. "Hey! What are you two doing in that truck?"

Martin turned to Virginia. It was up to her. She had a thoughtful look. Here we go again, Martin said to himself.

"It will take a moment, Corporal," Martin explained.

A phone was ringing inside. The corporal drew his gun, hollered to another soldier in the office and reached up for the handle on the door of the ambulance.

"What's that, Corporal?" Virginia said, pointing across Martin to the office. "That place is on fire!"

No sooner had she uttered the words than the office exploded in flames and the soldier inside ran out, yelling, "Fire!"

The corporal froze for a moment, hand on the door, fascinated by the flames. Then he gave a hoarse cry and ran for the nearest building.

"Let's get out of here!" Virginia cried.

Martin gunned the ambulance and they slid through the reservation entrance on screeching tires as they turned onto the highway.

In Avon Ridge they parked the ambulance on a side street and walked toward the center of town.

"They probably have an alarm out for this ambulance by this time," Virginia said.

"Us, too."

She nodded. "I wouldn't doubt it, if that little corporal has recovered from shock. We're not going to be able to stay here for long."

"What about renting a car?" he suggested.

"Renting?" She smiled at him. "That's a little naïve, don't you think? They'd easily trace us that way."

"I suppose so. Well, let's steal one. I've already been dead, so I guess it doesn't make any difference how I start out my new life."

"You sound bitter. Are you sorry I rescued you?"

"You know I'm not," he said. "It's just that I feel so

damned helpless. I don't understand it all and I'm so—so impotent."

"There's a car," she said, stopping and nodding to a new sedan parked in front of a residence. "It has a full gas tank."

"Now how can you tell that?"

"I just know."

"How are we going to get it started?"

"Come on," she said. "I just changed a couple wires at the ignition switch. All you need to do is push the starter."

"There you go again," he said, following her.

They got in the car, he pushed the starter button and the motor leaped to life.

They headed toward the business district, picked up the main street which became a highway on the outskirts. They were nearing the edge of town, driving within the speed limit so as to attract no notice, when Virginia tensed, put a hand on Martin's arm.

"Damn!" she said.

"What's the matter?"

"It's Dad."

"Where?"

"Right behind us."

Martin looked in the rear view mirror, saw nothing at first, then caught sight of a jeep as it passed a street light speeding toward them.

"Pull over," she ordered. "There's nothing else we can do."

Martin put the car to the curb and in a few moments the jeep slid to a stop in front of them, blocking the way. Martin's heart was beating wildly now; he wanted to run, yet knew it was useless. He hoped that in the impending battle of power Virginia would be the victor. Dr. Eric Penn got out of the jeep, came over to Virginia's side of the car, his grey eyes blazing in anger, his face livid.

"By what right——" he exploded, but Virginia interrupted.

"I told you how I felt," she said.

"But you've violated—" He put his hands to his head. "Never in our history has this happened. What do you think you're doing, Virginia? You've not only violated every rule but you've disobeyed your father."

"You went ahead despite my pleading," she said. "There were other ways."

"You've disgraced me, Virginia! Who is going to explain this to the Triumvirate? Who is going to account for it all? Not only have you brought back a human from annihilation, but you've used our power in a disgraceful show—that brick wall, that fire in the gatehouse office, that—that changing the wires . . ."

"Yes," she said calmly. "I know."

"Then—then?"

"Don't you suppose *I* have feelings?" she retorted. "I knew those manifestations would let you know where I was, but I thought perhaps you wouldn't care." Her lower lip quivered. "I thought this would show you how I felt as nothing else would." She looked at her hands clasped in her lap.

"There are those of your own kind," her father said reproachfully.

"But Dad! I found no one on my own plane. On this one I have found someone toward whom I respond."

"Him?" Her father looked directly at Martin.

"What's wrong with me?" Martin managed to say.

"I'm sorry, Virginia, but I'm going to have to ask you to return with me."

"And what about Martin?"

"Don't be a fool, Virginia. You know there is no hope for him." Then he added abjectly, "For all I know there may be no hope for you. If you would come now perhaps we could convince The Three."

"I'm sorry, Dad. I can't go with you."

"If only you had said something," he pleaded. "We could have provided someone. I never guessed you really felt this way."

"I told you."

"But it was too late!"

"I don't think it was, Dad."

"But how can this ever end?" Dr. Penn was beside himself in mixed grief, bewilderment and anger. "*They* will find you. There are many of them, you know. I will have to report this entire incident."

Virginia put fingers over her father's hand on the door of the car. "Don't report us right away, Dad. Please give us a little time."

He shook his head. "You've got him protected. How do I know what you'll do next? I must report you. I'm sorry, Virginia." He started to move away from the car. "I didn't expect a child of mine . . ."

He stopped talking and stood there for a moment, not moving. Martin looked intently at him, wondering what had happened.

"I'm sorry, Dad," Virginia said, opening the door. Her father fell to one side on the lawn beside the street. She got out of the car, walked up to the door of the nearest house.

Martin sidled over to where she had been sitting, took a look at Dr. Penn who was as one asleep on the grass.

"I guess I'm just a not-so-innocent bystander," Martin said when Virginia returned. "Would you mind explaining?"

"Later." The girl bent over, kissed her father on the forehead. "Good-bye, Dad," she said. Then she got in the car, told Martin to head out of town. There were tears in her eyes.

She wiped the last of the tears away when they were miles from Avon Ridge and had taken more than a score of turns on various roads to shake possible pursuit.

The night was cool. There was nothing but moonlight and the open road and the rush of wind past the car.

"Dad let his guard down when he was talking to me," she explained suddenly, slumping in her seat, leaning toward him and putting her head on his shoulder. "I didn't do the same. Otherwise he might have put me out and your envelope would have gone with me.

"I merely paralyzed his neural centers temporarily. All functions, except those necessary for living, such as breathing and the beating of the heart, were halted. He'll recover soon."

"What did you do at the house?"

"I told the people a man had fainted while talking to us. I said I didn't know his name but suggested they call the hospital or the police. Dad didn't need it, but I just didn't like the idea of leaving him there on the grass so lonely and —and unprotected."

She dabbed at her eyes again.

"Now he'll be really angry," she said. "I don't know what he'll do."

# 11

Among other things, the face of Managing Editor Lovett Wilson and his omnipresent cigar came to Martin's mind as he drove along the road with the girl at his side. An unreal road. An unreal girl. No, he could touch her if he wanted to. She was real. But everything was so disjointed, so crazy . . . Did the New York office think I'd run into anything like this, Willie?

And you, Chonkey. You ought to be with me. You'd have the time of your life photographing the things that have happened to me. Only nobody would believe it. Something for your morgue, Jimmy Simpson. Something for you to do research on. Put it in the file for good old *National Scene*. Tell Senior Editor Denton Myers to stand by with pad and pencil . . .

Then there was FBI man Kenneth Aldrich and General Walter Deems . . . Want to know what happened to Forrest Killian, General? If you promise not to laugh at me, I'll tell you: He was annihilated and the particles of his being were strewn through the cosmos. Do you believe that? I find it hard to believe myself, General. And then there was Dr. Merrill. Martin felt a sharp pang of regret about Dr. Merrill. He had liked him.

The crazy thoughts, the separating of the living from the dead, Bobby and his sphere, Virginia and her hazy eyes that he looked into once when they weren't hazy. Why did she bring me back? Why did she go against her father and her people? What people? Why? Why? Why?

Suddenly Martin pulled the car over to the side of the road and stopped.

"What are you doing?" Virginia said, sitting up in alarm.

"This is no good," he said firmly.

"Why?"

"That's exactly it," he said. "Why? That's all that's been running through my head. Why?"

"But someone will find us here," she said, looking up and down the road. "State police—or Father!"

"How can you expect me to go on like this, not knowing why these things are happening, not knowing whether I should report what I know to General Deems——"

"O my God, no!" she cried. "I'm sorry, Martin. I've been thinking so much about myself and what I ought to do I haven't given a thought to you. Reporting to General Deems would be the worst thing you could do. Can't you find a lane we can turn down? Then I will try to explain a few things."

Martin started the car, drove a short distance and turned off on the first byway. The lane went deep into a wooded area where bushes and branches scratched the side of the car. Eventually they came to a clearing where he stopped the car and turned off the lights.

"Well?" He looked at her, a face of even greater beauty in the soft moonlight, bright spots in the eyes that were the moon's reflection, full red lips made dark by the moonglow.

"Don't be backward," she said softly, putting a hand behind his head, bringing it toward her.

"I was under your spell once," he said, hesitating. The urge to take her in his arms nearly neutralized the memory of his awakening from her mental hold over him.

"You don't understand," she said. "I love you." She looked up at him with wide eyes, eyes without guile or mockery. Eyes of desire.

"Your explanation . . ."

"This is partly it, darling."

"No tricks!"

"Tricks? For heaven's sake, darling . . ."

The electric touch of her lips unleashed an overwhelming love for her in Martin. The kiss was long; it was unearthly and as ethereal as her eyes. It took them to between earth and the moon and there they hung in space between two worlds, alone with the silent stars, the warmth of their love emanating in every direction like the light of the sun, erasing the bitter chill of outer space. . . .

When he released her, he sat with her, stroking her hair, kissing her eyes, her nose. Once in a while she clung to him as if she were afraid he would run away. They said nothing.

"That," she said finally, "is not telling everything."

They lighted cigarettes and were silent again, listening to the faint sounds of the autumn night: a cricket near by, the crackle of dry leaves not yet fallen from branches as they brushed one against another in the light breeze. Then she spoke.

"About fifty thousand years ago," Virginia said slowly, "a man and a woman from the fourth planet of a star in the constellation your astronomers call Auriga came to Earth."

She looked up at the moon and studied its full face. "They were two people sent by their advanced culture to seek a planet where there was life. They were to colonize the planet and use the life they found there to help create more of themselves."

Virginia faced Martin. "They were not people as you would think of people, Martin. Millenniums ago they might have been like you and your kind. But in millions of years they had advanced so far beyond you that it is impossible for you to comprehend them, for their natural life-form is much different from yours now. For you to conceive it would be like trying to explain cybernetics to a savage—please don't get angry by the comparison. It's the only way I have of explaining." She laid a hand on his arm.

"Go on," he said.

"These two people found, much to their delight, an early world here. Europe was then a wilderness inhabited by hippopotamuses, elephants and mammoths, to say nothing of a few saber-toothed tigers. To their amazement, they also found a creature who resembled what they had looked like millions of years before. It was early man, a creature who was accustomed to squatting about an open fire and near a source of water."

She tamped the cigarette out in the ashtray. "The two travelers from the planet so far away—Capella Four—decided Earth was the world for them. They had searched many galaxies for such a place. They informed their parent civilization and landed here. They saw that it would be millions of years before the animal they had found—man—would evolve to the point they desired. They felt that he might not survive at all; he might not become the dominant life form. So they impregnated this animal with reasoning power.

"You, Martin, are a descendant of that animal. In you the reasoning power instilled in the first man is carried on as it has been through the years. We have kept your reasoning power alive, pushing you ahead of other life-forms. You have won out over other challenging life-forms because you were able to reason."

"But why did they do this?" Martin asked.

"These people were—are—immortal," she continued, as if he hadn't spoken. "They are still alive. From these two original people of ours have grown a society of Capellans numbering in the thousands, some living among you, but all living, thinking, growing side by side with your civilization, waiting for the day when they will return to live forever on Capella Four. For them these thousands of years that have passed since the first couple came here have been but a moment, considering their immortality."

"Why couldn't these people of yours reproduce on Capella Four?"

"There is no life-form such as yours there to be used," she said patiently. "Actually, the first animals found here resembling you were valueless. They did not possess enough reasoning power. They were like a radio set that was receiving no radio waves, although that's oversimplifying it. Once this reasoning power was instilled in these first men—oh, understand me, they had a little reasoning power, but not enough for us—you started to progress. You have evolved in the past fifty thousand years as far as you would have gone without us in two or three million years.

"So it was that the first two people from Capella decided to instill man with definite intelligence—a thought force. It was like growing a garden, you see. Your brain was the soil; our devices accelerated the growth of the seed we planted much as the sun would have helped grow a flower. Without the thought force field you would revert back to the early days—the pre-Neanderthal period. We nourished your reasoning power and it has grown as man has grown. It has been carried on to man's children and to his children's children, always kept alive by the power we supply it. I won't try to explain it. It would be like trying to explain what happens when a migrating bird makes its journey. It is a concept beyond physics and chemistry and radio. You have seen examples of the power of the thought force in what I have done.

"Each of you Earth people holds in his brain a fraction of the thought force that each of the Capellans possesses. The thought force in man is most vigorous at his most vigorous age—between eighteen and thirty-five. Do you follow me?"

Martin sighed. "I follow you, but I don't understand."

"Your progress has been fast, though history as you write it says it has been slow. Ours, Martin, was really slow. There were no outsiders around to help us. We didn't evolve for millions of years. But we have edged you forward. Eventually you might have been able to communicate with yourselves by sheer brain waves as we do."

"You are one of them, then?" Martin asked with a sinking heart.

"I was," Virginia replied. "But I am here now, a woman just as you are a man, endowed with what a woman is endowed with. . . . Does it bother you to know?"

"It—it will take some getting used to."

"Think of me!" Virginia said. "I've got to get used to you, too. Think of that."

"But——"

"Look," Virginia said. "In our own place, on our own plane where I come from, which I explained is co-existent with yours, we look at each other much as you and I do. There we have the same desires, the same feelings—there is sex there, too. Otherwise how could we reproduce? We are subject to the same natural laws as you people, except that they are vastly advanced."

"I was wondering about that."

"You needn't have. Of course it's *different,* from what I've been told." Martin could not see the blush because it was night.

"Naturally," he said drily.

Virginia laughed. "You *can* be jealous, can't you? Well, you needn't be. I have loved no one else."

"I still don't understand why these two people you talk about came here in the first place," Martin said.

"To grow a garden. To grow men's minds. When the garden has grown so much, then the harvest."

"Harvest?"

"Wars. Plague. This releases the thought forces from the new dead in tremendous quantities. It is this thought force released that is the ultimate goal of our people."

"You mean when people die in quantities, the thought force is released in concentration? Is that right?"

Virginia nodded. "The thought force so released is gathered much as microwaves would be gathered on a dishlike antenna. Our offspring benefit by this force. It is directed into and becomes part of their brains. Each of our children, as he or she is born, must have implanted in the brain the concentration of thousands of adult, ripe thought forces from men. Otherwise they would have no more thought force than you. They would be mortal and of relatively low intelligence, by our standards."

"You kill people to do this?" Martin asked in horror.

"You people kill yourselves," she said without emotion. "Occasionally we lend a hand when a sudden surge of thought force is necessary."

"It's ghastly!" He drew away from her.

"I suppose it would appear so at first glance."

"Then to you we are like—like cattle, like the animals we raise to eat!"

"Has anyone asked the cows and the pigs how they like what you are doing to them?"

"But that's different! They're dumb animals!"

"Have you ever thought of what you must be to us?"

"Then you are to me what I would be if I were to tell a sow that I had fallen in love with her!" he cried, shaken.

"Nonsense!" She lit a cigarette with a shaking hand. "If you changed yourself into a pig it is conceivable a sow might look attractive to you. But you haven't. The fact that I am here as Virginia Penn has no parallel in that thought. It so happens I am in love with you *even though I am aware of my other existence.* Could you do that with a sow? Doesn't that tell you that your analogy doesn't make sense?"

Martin was silent.

"I suppose it is tragic to you to think of all the wars and campaigns and terrible catastrophes from earthquakes to volcanic eruptions that have taken place merely to release the thought force. But mankind has grown with it as he was intended. He has harnessed nature. He has become a thinker. None of these things would have been possible without the seed planted by the first people from Capella—the star Alpha Aurigae.

"Your reasoning power has existed only through the courtesy of our people, much as your radio picks up its programs from the various radio waves you have invented—invented because the idea was implanted by us. We have, in a sense, kept the sun shining for you.

"You've heard the flashes of insight inventors sometimes have, the sudden discoveries, the waking of a man in the middle of the night with the answer to a problem he has tried to solve for years. These are implanted by us when we have felt you were ready for them, ahead of their logical discovery in what would have been your natural evolution. We have profited by your existence, using you while we have made possible the increasing numbers of you. Your civilization could not have progressed without us. Oh, you could have advanced to where you are in millions of years, but you certainly could not have done it in a mere fifty thousand years.

"We have not been idle as you have been growing. We have been at your sides, though you didn't know it. We have harvested some of you, let others of you go to seed. We have helped you progress. We have let you increase your population. Now we are waiting for word that the thousands of us who have been born during those thousands of years may go back to our star system.

"We let you invent the atomic bomb. We directed you toward its solution, so that those thousands at Hiroshima and Nagasaki could be wiped out so that several of our children could be imbued with their thought force heritage at once. We are now waiting for word whether or not we should let you use the fusion bomb—the H-Bomb—so that most of your two billion will be killed and release enough thought force for more than a hundred births, the last act before we leave your planet and head for home. We have been waiting for a long time. The children have not yet been conceived for this, however."

"How—how old are you?" Martin asked hesitantly.

"Twenty-three."

"Really?"

"What difference does it make how old I am *there?* It is the here and now that counts. I am twenty-three here. I was born here just like you. For all I know I may never go back because I have fallen in love with you and because of the things I've done. You heard what Father said."

"Superwoman loving Inferiorman."

"Don't say that, darling. It's not true."

"Not true?"

"I could not have brought you back if you had been just like other men. When you were annihilated and I started to bring you back you *helped* me. No other that I know among your numbers could have done that. What do you suppose I see in you, anyway?"

Martin opened his mouth to say something, but her cool fingers stopped him.

"Don't deny it, Martin," she said. "You know what I mean. You've felt it and thought about it, for I've seen it in your mind. You have a unique ability to penetrate others, to judge correctly their emotions, whether or not they will be receptive to what you have to suggest. You secretly pride yourself on this ability to see beneath the surface.

"In your mind I saw that at one time in your life you mentioned this ability to someone only to have that person shy away from you. You learned then to say nothing about it again. You learned it was wiser to pretend you were no different from anyone else."

"Lots of people have that ability," he said. "I'm not alone."

"Lots of people think they have it, Martin. But yours is the only true case I've seen. It is because of this thing that I find it possible to love you."

He studied her, wondering whether to believe her or not. "Are you trying to tell me I am like your people?"

She shook her head. "Not at all. You are merely an example of what your people will be like in the near future. If we are still here they will begin learning how to communicate with each other mentally. I knew you were different when you penetrated our minds to some extent. You didn't trust us—you knew something was odd about us as no one else has. You haven't trained this thing you have, otherwise you might have learned what we were right away. If trained, this talent would surprise you. You have to listen hard with your mind,

Martin; you have to project your thoughts and work hard at it. You might conceivably be able to move a ball on a table if you'd think about it hard enough. You certainly could do it with practice."

"All right," Martin said. "I'll admit I've thought about my intuition about people. Once I got a set of ESP cards and surprised myself with my high score. I've had it since I was a boy and I just thought I was lucky, that's all. But let's get back to you. Why are you and your father and brother on my plane?"

"There are many of us among you as human beings," she explained. "We are born, live and die just as you people do. It's a tour of duty to us. My mother, for example, asked to return to our plane and she died as a human so she could go back. That is where my father went each night when he visited the laboratory. We all took turns going back. We merely vanished for the time we were gone.

"You saw Bobby doing what you thought were magic tricks. Bobby is really a child. He had been warned not to make any display of that kind. But, as I say, he's still a child, comparatively speaking. When he did that bit of telekinesis, we all felt it and tried to get to him but you saw him and he stopped before we could do anything about it."

"I felt a cold wind then," Martin said. "I felt the same thing when your father disappeared." He laughed. "I guess there must be something in what you say about me."

"Of course there is. To go on, though. There are many of us in high places—and low places. It is up to us to shift public opinion, to incite wars and riots, to inflame hatreds. Many of our people have been the world's martyrs—and the world's most hated men."

"Hitler, I suppose?"

"One of the most recent, yes," she said. "There have been many in history. Genghis Khan, Hannibal, many emperors and kings. But not always. When one of us was not at the head of the government, when the time was ripe we merely dominated the individual who was."

"As you did me?"

"Worse, darling. I just suggested things to you, but we enslaved these others. You ought to read your history. There are many events which puzzle scholars but which are logical if thought of in terms of mental enslavement.

"You asked about what father and I were doing. We three —I'm including Bobby—are the earthly counterparts of our family. Actually, I have several brothers and sisters, in addition to my mother, on the other plane. Father was directed to solve certain biological problems for the advancement of

Yes! CHOOSE Any 3
All Full-Size
Full Length Books
SCIENCE FICTION FANS! Here's a bargain offer you just can't afford to miss. Take any 3 of the handsome, hard-bound, full-size volumes shown here — a $9.40 to $16.20 value — for only 99¢ and membership in the Science Fiction Book Club.
Why We Make This Offer
We make this offer to introduce you to the only Book Club that guarantees to bring you the best new science fact and fiction books every month — at a fraction of their price! Yes, as a member, you get these brand-new, full length books FOR ONLY $1 EACH — even though they cost $2.50, $3.00 and more in original publishers' editions.
You'll be proud to own and display these top-notch selections — each one jam-packed with unique adventures and fast-paced action! Each month's selection is described in advance. You take only the books you want — as few as four a year. No money in advance; no membership fees. You may cancel membership any time.
SEND NO MONEY
Just Mail Postcard Today!
Don't miss out on this bargain offer! Take your choice of any 3 of the new science fiction books shown here for only 99¢. Two are your gift books for joining; the other is your first selection. Mail the postcard — without money — now.
THE Astounding SCIENCE FICTION ANTHOLOGY
EARTH IS ROOM ENOUGH
ISAAC ASIMOV
THE BEST FROM FANTASY and SCIENCE FICTION
Omnibus of SCIENCE FICTION
Edmond Hamilton
THE STAR OF LIFE
Triad
A. E. van Vogt
THE WORLD OF Ā
THE VOYAGE OF THE SPACE BEAGLE
SLAN

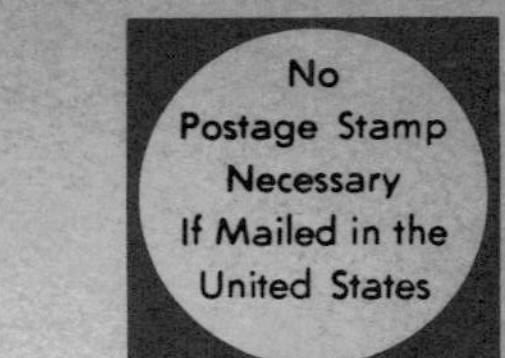


**B U S I N E S S   R E P L Y   M A I L**

First Class Permit No. 3 — Sec. 34.9 — P. L. & R. — Garden City, N. Y.

**Science Fiction Book Club**

**Garden City, New York**

your people, which he did. But someone of you thought of research on regeneration—you see? Your people are thinking more and more on their own.

"But we just could not allow regeneration. So Dad was worked into the position of heading up the project to stall it. Others, besides your Forrest Killian, discovered what Dad was doing. They have been annihilated in one way or another, for if regeneration were allowed there are too many other things you would discover too soon. Then there would be few casualties in battle. Since the growth of our group depends upon the release of concentrated thought force through the sudden death of thousands, we couldn't allow it. Now does that explain it all for you?"

# 12

Though it was a chilly night and Martin had only his suit coat to protect him, he opened the door of the car and stepped out on the soft ground, closing the car door behind him. He had to be alone. He had to escape those eyes of hers for a little while; the enormity of the thing she had told him had caused his head to ache.

He looked around the clearing. Thirty feet away there were trees, black giants reaching upward, their branches against the star-strewn sky like black lace in the heavens. There were bushes there, too, and more bushes and trees beyond them.

I could run, he thought. I could run to where the trees are and then beyond into the bushes. I could keep running and never look back and I'd never see her again. Then I could forget her and escape all this.

He leaned against the car and looked deep into the sky. He knew he could never do that. I guess I love you, Virginia, he said to himself. Else why do I stay? But why did you have to turn out this way? Why are you someone strange, someone from another world who says she loves me? Why couldn't you be a cute young thing without a brain in your head and I would have to take care of you? Or a secretary. A college girl, or maybe even a widow with kids.

*Because you are not an ordinary man.* The thought startled him and he wondered for a moment whether or not she had sent it to him, but then he knew she had not. Perhaps he was no ordinary man. Perhaps that is why he had never known a girl he could love before. He had been looking for someone —someone with ethereal eyes—someone who now sat in the car against which he was leaning.

Perhaps Virginia had asked herself the same question. "Why did I have to fall in love with a mortal man?" she might have asked herself. Perhaps her subconscious had given her the same answer.

Then there was the knowledge of all that she had said. The first man and woman from Capella, coming here to be catalysts in the accelerated development of the species they chose because it resembled their ancient forebears more than any other living thing on earth at that time.

So man hadn't been so smart after all! As a captive civilization and with his new intelligence he was able to survive better than the animals who suddenly had become lesser animals. Man was to become a creature of invention and quick progress, thanks to the Capellans. But why thank the Capellans? They gave the spark of knowledge to men and watched it grow as Virginia said, in a garden, only to cut him down, decimate him so the cultivated thought force would be released and caught by the Capellans, bloodthirsty creatures from out of space who stood around waiting for men to grow to maturity so they could annihilate them and gleefully sop up the thought force so released. . . .

No, I mustn't think of it that way. Virginia is right. We, with our slaughter of cattle, are doing the same thing, although it is to the nourishment of our bodies and not our brains primarily. If the intelligence levels are in the same ratio, there is no reason to look at it with revulsion. It is the survival of the fittest, Nature's oldest game, still going on with man being the beast of the forest and the Capellans the superior people, the hunters.

He shivered as the night air penetrated the suit coat. Then he felt a hand on his shoulder and he turned to see Virginia standing beside him, her eyes bright, her expression concerned.

"I'm all right," he said quietly. "I just wanted to think."

She stood there, not taking her hand away, and they both looked at the sky.

"Between those trees just ahead of us," she said, pointing to a star-filled space between two tall elms, "is Capella. It is in the constellation Auriga, almost on a level with the Pleiades at this time of the year."

He looked to where she was pointing in the eastern sky, saw a bright star near others in the constellation.

"It is a yellow star," she said. "It is like your sun in that respect, but it is not a dwarf. It is a giant star, fully a hundred times as big as your sun. One of the planets circling it will eventually be the home of the Capellans now on Earth. It is where my people want to be."

"What will happen to Earth men when the Capellans leave?"

"They will revert back to primitive ways," Virginia said gravely. "They haven't really progressed very far. It is only our presence that keeps them ahead of their time. It will be like turning off a radio broadcasting station; the radio set then responds only to local electrical disturbances."

"When are the Capellans going to leave?"

Virginia shrugged. "Who knows? Tomorrow? A hundred years from now? None of us knows. We have been waiting for word for years."

"What is going to happen to us? You and me?"

"Do you love me?" She looked up at him.

He took her in his arms. "I will always love you."

"Then we will have each other."

He kissed her tenderly. "Aren't you afraid?"

"Not with you."

"But if your people are as powerful as you say, they should have no difficulty finding us."

"There are no more emanations to guide them," she said. "I am no longer protecting you with a force-field envelope. I have blocked off that part of me that is alien to you; I have lost my Capellan identity voluntarily. I am now only a woman. To my own people I would now appear as one of you."

"But couldn't one of these Capellans be floating around us right now?"

She smiled. "I could sense one and so could you if you thought much about it."

"No more miracles, then?"

"We're on our own. If I violate the rules and interfere with the natural workings of your society again it will be like a beacon light to them. We'd be discovered at once."

"They all know about us, do you think?"

"I doubt there is a Capellan who doesn't. They'll be watching for us everywhere. All we have to do is be careful. You will learn to identify them by intuition, I will tell you which persons are Capellans if you are in doubt. Until you learn to sense them as you wondered about Dad, Bobby and me, I suggest we stay together as much as possible."

"I won't let you out of my sight," he said, grinning. "But will they *do* anything? Can they read our thoughts?"

"That is interfering in your society. They can't and won't do it unless you are asleep or nearly asleep and then only in an emergency, such as back at Park Hill."

"They know who we are, what we look like."

She nodded. "I'm afraid they do."

"What will they do if we're found out?"

"I don't know. We must stop them from finding us. They are prone to error just as human beings are. They cannot penetrate a disguise, for example, unless they suspect it is a disguise."

"Well, that's something." He looked at her blonde hair. "You could dye your hair. I could get a crew cut and start smoking a pipe."

"That's a start. But where are we going to go?"

"I know an abandoned cabin in the Wasatch Mountains near Salt Lake City. Think we could make it? We could get a different car. Police are probably looking for this one."

"You're the boss," she said, punching him playfully in the arm. "It's about time you took over."

They sat in the clearing through the last dark hours of the morning, occasionally starting the motor and heater to keep warm in the encroaching chill of the predawn October day.

They used the time by logically examining their chances of reaching the cabin Martin remembered in Utah.

"When I was in the army in nineteen forty-three, I was stationed near Great Salt Lake taking overseas training," Martin explained. "I discovered this cabin on one of the long marches our unit made near there. It was an overnight bivouac and, after the tents had been pitched, I went on an exploration tour of the area near the camp. Everybody laughed at me. 'Haven't you had enough hiking today?' they asked. One guy said, 'He's found a home, Martin has. He's bucking for something.'

"I guess I was a character to them for I liked to hike. I found this cabin in a small ravine. It was empty and forlorn looking. Probably a relic from gold-rush days."

"Maybe some early Mormon hunter built it," Virginia said.

"Could be." He looked at her and said, "It's not much, Virginia. Hand-hewn logs. Small windows. I don't think there's a nail in it anywhere. Maybe it isn't even there any more."

"I don't care. We'll make it our home for a while—if we make it—if it's still there."

"We can't stay around here."

Martin examined the contents of his pockets: Travelers Checks, about twenty-five dollars in cash, identification, initialed cigarette lighter, cigarettes. Virginia had nothing.

They decided to cash the Travelers Checks, then Martin could burn his identification papers, throw away his cigarette lighter. They could not afford to take a chance.

"When I do that it will be like starting a new life," he said. "Good-bye, Martin Enders, hello—who?"

"Hmmm." Virginia pursed her lips. "I like Steve. It has a masculine ring. We'll have to call you Steve—Steve Miller. That's not an unusual name. There must be thousands of Steve Millers in the world today. Do you like it?"

"It's all right. Now I'll have to pick one for you. Let's see. How about Dorothy?"

She shook her head emphatically. "It can't be Dorothy. That was my mother's name."

"Nancy?"

"So-so."

"Last name?"

"Miller, of course."

"Of course." He squeezed her hand.

"It was only yesterday in the washroom that I nearly hit Dr. Merrill, you had me so souped up against him," Martin said as the first faint light of day appeared. "It seems it ought to be a week ago."

"And I thought you would remain in the trance I had you in until the danger was over," Virginia said. "But I knew something would happen. I just felt it."

"Yesterday I was pretending to work for *National Scene* magazine doing a story about a research scientist in a government project while I was really investigating this same man for the Counter-Intelligence Corps and General Deems. Today what am I?"

"It's my fault," she said softly. "I feel it is somehow. There should have been something I could have done, but there wasn't. Dad knew about you and hoped to discourage you without arousing suspicion, but you wouldn't discourage. When he learned you had seen Bobby, he wanted to be sure you didn't know too much, so you had to come to live with us so he could watch you and you could be convinced Bobby was just a normal boy and that somehow you only imagined what you had seen him do. But when he learned about your connection with General Deems and when he discovered Dr. Merrill had been talking to you about Forrest Killian, then it was too late."

"I wish I had known," he said. "Then I could have avoided it—or could I have?"

"No, in any case. If you had known you would have done something aggressive and it would have ended the same way, only sooner. Forrest Killian was aggressive."

"Were you in love with Forrest Killian?"

She laughed. "Of course not." Then she became grave. "I just didn't like what was happening to him. He was a likable fellow but he, too, entered the trap from which there was no exit. There have been others. I'd rather not talk about them."

Martin turned the ignition key Virginia had taken the precaution of creating earlier, stepped on the starter. "I only wish there were some way to combat the Capellans," he said. "I feel as if I'm running away when I might be doing something."

"I'm sure you would try to escape a firing squad," she said. "Believe me, they don't care about Martin Enders. You were annihiliated once; you could be disposed of as easily again. I might not be around to bring you back the next time."

"I'd still like to talk to the fellows at *National Scene.*"

"They'd laugh at you."

"And General Deems. He ought to know."

"He'd laugh, too. Don't you see, darling? They wouldn't believe you and by the time you got around to proving anything you'd be dead."

"But there *must* be a way to defeat them!"

"Why defeat them? The Capellans are a benign influence. With them gone, so would be man's reasoning power. If it weren't for them, man wouldn't be where he is. If they chose to do so, they could send man back to Neanderthal days any time."

"But I can't accept letting them continue the wars, the plagues, the killing for their selfish purpose of self-perpetuation. After all, man has a right to his own natural evolution without this needless bloodshed caused by the Capellans."

"Pretty in theory, darling, but hardly practical. They happen to be in the driver's seat."

He put the car in gear, started it rolling out of the woods.

"All right," he said. "We'll try it your way for a while. If we make it to Utah, perhaps I can think of something."

"You're welcome to try," Virginia said. "But I think it's a lost cause."

# 13

For a long time the old man stood on the crag of weathered rock, leaning against the lone juniper tree, peering down into the valley, occasionally spitting a stream of yellow juice which splattered on lower slopes.

Wisps of clouds scudded low in the sky as if they were left behind by some greater formation and were hurrying to catch up. The sun was warm on the terraced red ledges of the foothill ridges and the valley that swung in a slow bend to the north.

A gentle breeze every now and then tucked at the man's denim shirt sleeves, played with the limp brim of the man's battered hat, but he did not take his eyes off the tiny cabin in the valley, although it was almost hidden from view because it was in a ravine down which rain must have rushed from the near-by ridges in the spring; it was a wonder it had never been washed away.

After a while the man left the tree, stretched, took another chew of tobacco and, skirting the striated outcropping, went plowing down the side of the hill, leaving a haze of hovering dust to be caught by fresh winds.

He was a small man, an old man whose tobacco-stained white beard fell to his chest and was sometimes caught by his combined motion and the wind to fly to one side and then the other.

With unconscious skill he avoided the deep layers of detritus, moving with ease over loose stones around boulders and through stands of piñons. His quick blue eyes never left the cabin.

"There's someone," Virginia said, looking up from her chair and dropping her darning into her lap.

"I felt it, too," Martin said. "It isn't one of them, is it?"

"I don't think so."

Both went to the cabin doorway and, looking up the slope of Tessie Valley, saw the figure moving down it, the plume of dust that rose behind him as he worked toward the greener plateau at the top of the ravine. He disappeared from their sight behind the clumps of young cottonwoods at the edge of the gulch.

"He'll be coming over in a few minutes," Martin said. "If he's not one of them, I wonder what he wants."

"If he's all right he'll be our first visitor," Virginia said. "We ought to have a welcome mat."

"I don't trust anybody. I wish he weren't coming," Martin declared.

Virginia laid a hand on his arm. "You've changed, darling," she said. "Don't. I liked you as you were."

"But I keep thinking——"

"Don't think, then. Don't try to carry the weight of the world on your back, Martin. After all, we've got to live out our lives you know. Start worrying like that and you won't be around very long."

He walked away from the door, left her standing there.

"What about what's in those?" he said, gesturing toward a small stack of newspapers. "Even you admit there's something going on."

"But I don't fret about it," she said, coming over to him and putting her arms around him, locking her hands on his chest. "Dad's dead. But that doesn't mean he's gone. They no doubt removed him because he became so involved in what was going on at Park Hill. Now they can hamper the project some other way—mental possession to block thinking down a specific avenue that would lead to discovery of the secret of regeneration, for example. It's been done before."

"Not a line about what *really* happened," Martin said.

"The military wouldn't let them say anything."

"What about your brother?"

"Bobby?" Virginia shrugged. "He'll take care of himself somehow."

He turned to her. "It seems so strange. Here your father is dead and you don't seem much to care."

"We've been through that. He isn't dead. He is only now really alive, unhampered by a physical being in your sense. He has, in a way, shuffled off his mortal coil for something better."

"Is it better?" he asked bitterly.

"Not without you," she said, kissing him lightly.

"But what about the others? You admit it's strange so many of your people are dying."

"I'll admit it has me worried. But perhaps it is only that now I'm much more aware of it; I keep looking for their names in the newspaper. The same number may have died right along, only there was no reason before for my thinking it anything but natural."

"I hear our friend."

They walked again to the doorway.

"Anybody to home?" the old man yelled down from the crest of the ravine wall a hundred yards away. He was a bright, sunlighted figure of a man who now took off his hat and scratched his head with the hand that held it.

They waved to him.

"Come on down," Martin cried.

"That I will. That I will." With amazing agility for an old man, white beard scrambled down the steep slope, jumped across the rivulet in the shallow and ambled up to them.

"Evenin' folks," he said.

"Won't you come in?" Martin said, stepping to one side of the door. "It's not much of a place yet, but you're welcome."

"Don't mind if I do," the old man said, coming forward with an extended hand. "My name's John Collins, though most folks call me Toby, I guess on account of I'm always a-chewin' terbaky. Been doin' it since I was a kid." He spat a blob into a clump of grass.

"I'm Steve Miller," Martin said, shaking the hand. The hand was firm. "This is my wife, Nancy."

"Pleased to meet you, ma'am," Toby said, doffing his hat.

"Come in, Mr. Collins," Virginia invited.

"Rather you'd call me Toby," he said, going through the doorway. "Say, you've gone and fixed this place up. Used to pass this way pretty often and once I thought of movin' in. Now I wish I had of."

"That's Nancy's handiwork," Martin said, following him inside.

"A woman's a mighty handy thing to have around, son. Us old coots don't have a way with frilly things like they do. You're mighty lucky, young feller, to have a girl like Nancy. Yep, mighty lucky. And so purty, too." He smiled and the white teeth shone brightly in the red, weathered face.

"Thank you, Toby," Virginia said. "Can I offer you something? Tea? Coffee? We don't have anything stronger."

Toby sat down in a wooden chair at the table, slapped his thigh and laughed. "Now what made a thing like that pop into your head? Will you answer me that? I ain't touched a drop of anythin' stronger'n tea in nigh onto ten years."

Virginia stirred up the fire in the small cookstove and put on a teakettle.

"Where you folks from?" Toby asked, spitting into the fireplace.

Martin looked closely at the man. There was nothing suspicious in his makeup; it seemed a logical question.

"I'm on a sabbatical from the university," Martin said. "Nancy and I thought we'd rough it out here for a while. I'm a geology teacher and we thought we might collect a few specimens around here."

"Knew a fellow out here once who dug up old bones for a museum back East. Great country for that, they say. May be I can help you. I know every cranny in the state of Utah and every lizard by its first name. Danged if I don't."

"And where do you live?" Virginia asked.

"A likely question, ma'am. A likely question." His eyes twinkled. "I have so many places I set down in I don't know which to call home. My best place is on the other side of Three Forks."

"You're a long way from home, Toby."

"Heard tell you folks was a-holin' up out here. Thought I'd come out personal to see what you looked like."

"Where did you hear that, Toby?" Martin asked.

"It's all over Three Forks," Toby said. "Folks there allow as how it's downright funny you two comin' in together all the time. You scared to stay here by yourself, ma'am?"

"No," Virginia said. "We just want to spend as much of our year together as possible."

"Wall, now, that's real purty, ain't it? Yep, that's what I'd call sure, real purty. You mind what I say, son. You're a lucky one, all right. Mind if I take off my shoes? My feet's a-killin' me."

"No. Go ahead," Martin said.

Virginia poured three cups of tea and set a plate of sweet rolls on the old table.

Toby took off his engineer's boots, wiggled his sock-covered toes. "This place is better'n mine now," he said. "Windows are clean, floor's been swept. I could have all that if I'd of married. But I couldn't stay in one spot long enough to get a woman to take my courtin' serious. It wasn't 'cause I wasn't handsome. No, sir, not old Toby. I was a high flyer and had a way with the girls. Would you believe that, ma'am?"

"Yes, I would believe it," Virginia said. "You still could sway the ladies, I'll bet."

"Now, ain't that nice! Right nice of you, ma'am. Now, if your husband wouldn't mind, I'd like to be sayin' you're just the kind of girl I used to go for. That nice black hair, those pretty blue eyes. You ought to let your hair down, really you ought, ma'am. It don't look just right up in a bun the way it is."

Martin lighted his pipe, inhaled the smoke.

"Chewin' is much better'n smokin', mister," Toby said, turning to Martin. "Where'd you learn to do that? Never saw a pipe smoker draw in the smoke exactly like that before. You just change from cigarettes?"

Martin brought the pipe out of his mouth slowly, let his hand fall with it. Virginia rose from her chair.

"Why do you ask that?" Martin said, eying the old man who returned the steady gaze.

"Thought that was it," Toby said. "That sure goes to show what a man will get out of just lookin' at things. I'd of never learned that out of a book." He dunked part of a roll in his tea, munched it with gusto.

Martin chanced a look at Virginia, but she did not seem too concerned. He had felt nothing out of the way with Toby, but the man did have a way of putting things bluntly—and correctly.

Toby took up his cup and made a sucking noise as he drew in the hot tea. He set it down again.

"You're probably aimin' to chink this place, ain't you? I can see holes that are sure going to need it when the winter wind starts blowin'. If you need help, I'll be glad to lend a hand. Want to be right neighborly. Everybody ought to be that way."

"I'd appreciate a hand," Martin said. "How can I get in touch with you?"

Toby laughed. "Oh, I'll be around. I'll just drop in once in a while. You just wait and see. Yep, you just wait and see."

Toby finished his tea, brushed his lips with a shirt sleeve that gave evidence of having been used this way before. After he had taken a fresh chew of tobacco and thanked them for their hospitality, he left the cabin. He turned at the top of the ravine and waved to them with his hat. Then with his customary alacrity, he strode from sight.

"Well, what do you make of him?" Martin asked, leaning against the doorjamb and idly watching the spot where the old man had disappeared.

"He could be doing as I am," she said. "I've blocked off my Capellan identity. As I've said, to a Capellan I'd appear, both outwardly and inwardly, a woman of this world. I was born as any Earth child, you know, except that I existed before that time."

She cleared the table, dumped the cups and saucers into a pan, emptied the teakettle water on them. "Toby could be holding his real identity from us. Capellans do not do this habitually, since there is no reason. But under these circumstances, he might be, if he is a Capellan," she declared.

"There's no way of telling, then." He sighed, turning into the cabin to help her.

She flashed him a smile as he came near. "Stop worrying, Martin. Remember the first time you kissed me?"

He took her head in his hands. "Sorry to be so tragic, Virginia. I'd just hate to lose you, that's all. As for remembering when I first kissed you, how could I ever forget the Twenty-third MP Battalion and what they did for us at Park Hill?"

"Why can't you forget, darling?"

"Because." He brushed her lips lightly with his, then drew her head to his, hard. Her arms went around him and he could feel the dampness of her hands through his shirt.

He watched her wash dishes, then leaned against the table, a towel in his hand. His gaze went from habit to the window and the wonderland beyond with its green grass on each side of the small stream that disappeared behind the face of a large wall of rock. There were frogs and lizards side by side out there and if they were quiet they could hear the trickling and gurgling of the tiny mountain stream.

It was an ideal spot. Up the ravine on the plateau he had camped with an army unit once and the men with him thought it was strange that he would explore the area. He had ventured to the gulch then and had seen the cabin for the first time, wondering whose it was and who had built it. He had not thought then that he would some day be living in it. He might have imagined that if he had tried, but he could never have imagined the circumstances under which he would come to it.

Yes, if it had not been for the ever-present danger of discovery, it would have been an idyllic spot, a lush setting for two lovers, something out of a Technicolor movie: the greensward of the valley floor, the bright, clear stream, the majesty of the mountains all around with their snow-topped peaks often lost in the clouds.

The last contact with the contemporary world had been with the car they had left five miles away in a small glen, for the people of Three Forks seemed not of this age; they were not touched by the hand of shutter-clicking, heavy-spending tourists—there were too many publicized attractions near by. When they walked the few miles down the stream to the village for their supplies, bought with the money from the cashed Travelers Checks, the people looked at them curiously, but not hostilely, and had offered unquestioning co-operation.

But then came Toby, small, white-bearded Toby who evidently knew the people at Three Forks. It was conceivable he was an emissary of the villagers, chosen by them because of his familiarity with the area and, more probably, because he would be direct and unashamed to ask his questions. Toby might be a man who, by virtue of his ramblings through the valleys and byways, felt he had a right to know who was living in the places he frequented.

But could he have been so astute?

"Penny for your thoughts, darling. You've been dreaming out that window for nearly five minutes."

"Oh, the usual," Martin said, turning to the dishes to dry them. "I guess the trouble with me is I've never had to hide from anyone. I've always been the hunter, a hunter for facts, ideas, news. It's against my nature to do this kind of thing, to run away from something and someone. I can't get used to it."

"Give yourself time, Martin. You're just too honest. You've always done what your conscience has decreed is right. Now you're in an impossible situation and you can't believe that it is impossible."

"It's that Toby," he said. "I don't trust him. His remarks about your hair, for example, as if he knew you had dyed it and made it into an upsweep. And that business about my pipe, as if he knew I had changed from cigarettes."

"He explained that pretty well, I think, the way you inhale. In all his travels, Toby probably has become a good judge of men and prides himself on noticing things like that. As far as my hair is concerned, I agree with him. I think it would look better down. I'd wear it that way, if it weren't for——"

Martin grunted. "For the Capellans. Star people who came here fifty-thousand years ago, fashioned an animal called *homo sapiens* and used him and now they're through with him."

"Why do you say they're through with him?"

"You know. You've told me yourself the Capellans are leaving their Earth existences, going back. What else can you assume from that?"

"You're right, I suppose. I should have kept track all along; then I would know whether or not the number who have died of heart attacks, like father, and the myriad other diseases, means anything." She paused for a moment. "But there is one thing, Martin."

He looked at her.

"*I* did not start it all."

"Of course not, darling. I'm not blaming you."

"I think," she said, crossing the room to a box under the bed, "that it's about time we opened the bottle." She withdrew a quart of wine. "This will do both of us good."

A harvest moon rode high in the heavens, shining brightly on the mountain stream, turning it into a ribbon of twisting, shimmering silver. A gentle breath of night air wafted the thin plume of smoke from the cabin chimney across the ravine to the plateau and it glided wraithlike up the valley.

Inside the cabin the fading embers in the fireplace frequently burst into temporary flame when wood, turning completely to ash, gave way to weight above it, sending sparks up the chimney as it fell and giving to the room a fitful, brief splash of eerie light.

The two of them lay asleep on the bed; the wine had hastened their slumber and made their sleep deep. They did not often move.

*It was only when Toby spoke softly that Martin stirred ever so slightly.*

*"You were plenty obligin'," Toby said quietly. "Plenty obligin' on the first time around. I didn't put you out none."*

*"No," Martin said, sitting up. "You didn't put us out."*

*"You wanted to be real friendly-like."*

*"Of course we wanted to be friendly."*

*"And to be real friendly you've got to be real truthful. Anybody knows that. Now ain't that right?"*

*Martin nodded. "That's right. Right as rain." That was silly. Pretty soon I'll be talking like the old duffer.*

*"If you was a true friend, you'd help me if I was in trouble." Toby gave him a quick look. "Wouldn't you now?"*

*"Yes. I would help you if you were in trouble."*

*"See? We agree on everything, don't we?"*

*"Sure." Toby was all right. He was a friend. He was a warm, alive old man. And a very nice guy to know.*

*"Well, if we're goin' to be real friends, we got to be honest with each other. Are you sure I can trust you, mister?"*

*"Certainly." What was the old guy getting at? Of course Toby could trust him. Why, Virginia . . .*

*"Eh? What was that?"*

*The image of Toby blurred and Martin had trouble concentrating on his eyes.*

*"Never mind, son. You and I, we'll get along, won't we?"*

*"We'll get along." That was better.*

*"We've known each other for years."*

*"For years?" Had he really known him that long?*

*"For years. Of course we have. You remember." Toby was smiling. The way he always smiled. Martin remembered now.*

*"Old friends that we be, we know each other through and through."*

*"Yes."*

*"We never had no secrets from each other."*

*"No, we never kept any secrets from each other." Of course not. Toby was an old friend. A friend from way back.*

*"You know my name."*

*"I know your name."*

*"What is it?"*

*"Toby." How ridiculous. Toby not knowing his own name.*

*"And what's your name?"*

*"Martin." How silly of Toby not to remem—*

Martin screamed with the sudden smash of light against his eyes, against the whirling figure at his side and suddenly something clicked inside his brain and he saw, emerging from a dream, that Toby had somehow entered the cabin.

"What the hell . . . !" He started to rise. Something forced him back.

"Stay back!" Virginia ordered.

It was then that he saw her standing against the wall, her breath coming fast, her eyes fierce and determined. She did not move.

He turned to Toby, saw him standing, frozen to a spot on the floor, equal determination in his blazing blue eyes.

Then he became aware of the tug of war, the exchange of power, the pulsations in the air that glowed and died and flickered like neon, the breath of hot wind that smote him and the hard, unyielding edge of something invisible that he could touch in front of him. The heat of it made him draw back in alarm.

The room resounded to the clashing of wills that slipped and slid and held and gave, the areas of combat emanating a radiance that lighted the room. The two Capellans stood, their eyes whipping at each other, the house creaking and groaning under the unleashed forces that battled each other within.

# 14

Sweat was rolling down the old man's face into his beard. Martin turned frantic eyes to Virginia and he saw her pale face, her lips a bloodless line, desperation in her eyes. Her fingernails dug into the bark of the logs at her side and her fingers were white; the muscles of her forearm were distended with strain, her breasts rose and fell rapidly as she fought for breath. Toby's rasping breath answered hers.

With a cry, Martin hurled himself at the man, but the impenetrable wall between did not yield and he bounced back helplessly to the foot of the bed, clawing at the fringe of the field.

Suddenly the old man started to shake as if in a chill. Then his hoarse respiration seemed to rip his throat and he moved, wild-eyed, staggering backward as if from blows.

"You—can—return—me," he cried shrilly, gasping for breath. "But—*they*—will—be—back."

Virginia moved from the wall and the air quieted.

"Thank you," Toby whispered, stopping his backward flight and leaning against the table to keep from collapsing. His white hair was disheveled, his eyes bloodshot. He still had difficulty with his breath.

"If I go—I'll tell them—where," he managed to say. "You can't—you can't stand against them all. They'll—they'll kill him . . ."

"They'll kill me first," Virginia retorted.

The old man sank to a chair. He was getting control of himself; his breath was less labored.

"You are disgustingly like an Earth mother guarding her young," he said.

"Why did you come here?" Virginia stood in the center of the room, facing him.

"I wasn't sure," Toby said. "You had blocked yourself so well I couldn't be sure. I had to come back. I knew I could discover the truth through your friend."

"Do they all know?"

"We've all been warned and everyone is looking—everyone left."

"So it is true!"

Toby looked at her in surprise and then grinned feebly. "I saw your papers. I thought you would be aware of it."

"And now that you know about us, what were you to do?"

"He," Toby said, indicating Martin with a vague movement of a hand, "is to die. Then you are to come back."

"So you came to kill him."

"If he turned out to be Martin Enders, yes."

"I thought your accent was phony, Toby," she said. "How long have you had it?"

"I've got along with it for years and nobody has complained."

"What reason do they give for wanting to kill Martin?"

"So he will not reveal what he knows, though I don't think anybody would believe him. But that's only the secondary reason. The main one is to get you back. They can't understand why you have acted this way."

Virginia turned to look at Martin. "I can tell you why, Toby." Her eyes glistened. "I happen to love this man."

"Love on this level?" Toby was incredulous. "Why do you stoop to a thing like that? He is just an ordinary man."

"He is not just an ordinary man."

"I saw nothing unusual about him," Toby said.

"I say he is *more* than an ordinary man."

"He must be," Toby said sarcastically. "I suppose you're going to tell me he has no atavistic tendencies."

"If he has, they are under control. His mind is much better than average, his extrasensory perception is highly developed."

"Unwarlike, eh?" Toby looked at Martin curiously. "Then what must he have thought of our little demonstration?"

"Have you forgotten that it may not be over?"

Toby snorted. "You are the one who is warlike, Virginia Penn. It is evident you have lived too long among these people. Have you forgotten your own kind?"

"My people have forsaken me," she said angrily, turning back to him. "Instead of letting us alone, they have sent all of you out to hunt us down!"

"You cannot forget your birth. You are not one of them."

"I wish I were!"

"Oh, come, now——"

"We are too complacent, too condescending, too sure of ourselves as a people. We are ethnocentrics. The Greeks and the Romans had a word for strangers, for people not like themselves. It was 'outsiders.'"

"It is our history, Virginia. If it weren't for the Earth people we could not propagate ourselves."

"But is there no end? Must we always be this way?"

Toby got up from his chair to come over to her, but Virginia waved him back.

"You keep sitting there, Toby. I don't trust you."

He sat down again. "As you wish. But to answer your question, do you think Earth people have advanced far enough to be released to continue in time on their own?"

"But we have been responsible for their wars, their plagues, the devastations."

Toby shrugged. "There are others among us far better to answer questions like that than I. I merely did what I was bid in trying to find you."

Virginia came over to sit on the bed with Martin.

"Why should they want me back? Since I've been so reactionary, I should think they'd be glad to get rid of me."

"I don't know, Virginia. If you were up to me, I'd say they would be better off forgetting you. But we all have been told what to do. The Triumvirate decides that. You know that."

She gave him a dark look. "I could send you back."

"I really believe you could. But what good would it do? If my Earth body dies here, I go back and others will find you, those still living on Earth. It would not take more than five minutes, I should say."

"I suppose you're right." Virginia put a hand on Martin's arm.

At that moment Martin felt a blast of cold air and looked at the old man in alarm. Instantly Virginia was on her feet. The disappearing form of the old man shimmered uncertainly for a moment in the dim light of the room, then settled back into solidity again.

"You *are* tricky, Toby. Now stay there like that, if you please, until I figure this out."

"There's no figuring to do, Virginia. You had better come back with me."

"I am not leaving Martin Enders."

"All right, then," Toby said disgustedly. "I give you my promise that nothing will happen to Mr. Enders. Now will you come with me?"

She looked beseechingly at Martin. "I don't know what to do, Martin," she said. "I can't just stay here now that he knows. If he leaves he will inform the others and they will come back as he says and kill you. There will be nothing I can do about that. I cannot keep him here permanently. He will escape somehow. If I destroy him, the other part of him goes back."

Martin stirred uneasily. He had been fascinated by the drama and could see now the futility of resistance. He had accepted the role of noncombatant from necessity; he did not like doing nothing about it.

"Perhaps you could come back," Martin suggested. "Surely when they learn how you feel they will let you come back. They *must* let you return."

Virginia turned cold, blue eyes toward the man. "I will go with you, then, on condition that you guarantee that I return."

Toby laughed. "How could I assure you what they'll do?"

"You could tell them you gave me your promise."

"Why should I?"

Virginia was silent. She looked away from him, studied the warped wooden floor for a long time. Toby looked at her in amusement.

"You *must* be in love with him," he commented.

Suddenly the girl's crafty eyes met his. "I am stronger than you are, Toby. I have proved that."

The smile faded. "Yes," he said hesitantly. "I will grant you that. But it doesn't mean you can use it to advantage."

"It so happens that it does, Toby," Virginia was more sure of herself now.

"You think so?"

"Unless you promise that I will return, I will hold you here as you are, in your Earth body, as long as I can. I will send Martin out to get food for me, none for you. You will starve slowly, Toby. It will take some time, of course. Perhaps I will give you something to eat to keep you barely alive. Then you won't be able to escape. How does that strike you?"

"What could you possibly gain by that?" It was plain Toby did not like the prospect.

"It is evident the Capellans are getting ready to leave this planet. That way you will be unable to accompany them."

"They would not leave without me!" Toby was a little frantic; his voice was shrill.

"Shall we try it and see?" Virginia smiled pleasantly.

"But when they leave," Toby said. "When they leave, Martin will . . ."

Virginia nodded. "I know. But at least they will not have killed him."

"No! I have looked forward for years to the journey." The old man's hands trembled as he talked. Then he threw them in air in dismay. "All right, *all right!* I promise. You will return." He seemed to go to pieces with this announcement, burying his head in his hands.

Virginia's fingers tightened on Martin's arm and they looked wistfully at each other.

"There is no other way," she said softly. "I will be back as soon as I can. Don't worry. And don't leave here!"

"All right, darling," he said. He ran his hands up her arms to her shoulders and a moment later they were in each other's arms.

"Remember," he said, his mouth an inch from her ear. "Remember, when you're back there, that I love you. That I will be waiting for you."

"I will, darling. I promise," she whispered back.

"What's it like—back there?"

She shook her head and her cheek, as it brushed his, was warm. "I can't tell you," she said. "It's—it defies description. But please don't worry."

When he let her go, he could see, by the light of the dying fire, that her eyes were rimmed in tears. She kissed her fingers, put them to his lips. They were cool.

"Good-bye, darling," she said. Then she turned to Toby. "You first." Her voice was gruff.

They sat on the bed, Martin holding her hand, watching Toby. There was an eddy of icy air and the old man faded from view. Martin then turned to Virginia, saw her profile, the nicely modeled chin, the full lips, the pert nose—and then with a heavy heart he felt frigid air as she faded. The fingers that had held her hand moved together, clutching only air.

It was suddenly very cold in the cabin.

The sun was a blazing hole in the October sky. It shone on jutting rocks in the ravine, reflecting their brilliant colors. It was caught shimmering in the water of the stream, water that was never clearer.

From where Martin stood at the top of the ravine he could see the curving stand of pines, the flat profile of the mountain, the timbered steppes of the jagged range. He could hear the rattle of cottonwood leaves, the sigh of the wind in the pines.

It was beautiful. Ironically beautiful, for it reminded him of Virginia. The thought of her filled him with nostalgia for the immediate past when all he needed to do was reach out his hand and he touched her.

A thousand times in the past few days he had looked for her when a shadow caught his eyes, when a twig fell from a tree, when a stone, loosened from its place on the side of the ravine, tumbled to the stream. But she was never there.

On this, the fourth day since she had gone, he determined to try to help pass the time by strenuous activity. Perhaps if he worked hard he might sleep, he thought, for in the face of her expected return, slumber had become an elusive thing.

He returned to the cabin, took a pail to the stream and filled it with water. Back in the cabin he set to work washing it down. That was the first project. When he finished that, he was going to chink it. The old man had been right about the crevices; they needed to be filled in before winter.

He was in the middle of scrubbing down the floor when, with a surge of elation, he felt a characteristic coldness. He sensed it was she behind him and he was about to turn when he thought; What if it isn't Virginia?

In panic, he whirled around.

Virginia was there and he rose from his work to go to her in joy. It was the look on her face that stopped him.

"What's happened?" he asked in growing alarm. Her eyes were listless, her face ashen. Her shoulders sagged. "What have they done to you?"

"They have done nothing." Virginia stood there looking at him with detachment. Her voice was weary.

"They have, too!" He approached her.

Virginia stepped back.

"No, Martin. It's no use."

He stopped, thunderstruck. Surely, they must have done something to her to cause her to be this way. They were exercising control over her . . .

"This can't be you. You couldn't have changed so."

She smiled bleakly. "I *have* changed, Martin. I am a Capellan. I will always be a Capellan. I belong with my people."

"But I thought——"

"That was impossible." There was an awful finality in the words. "I loved you. I still love you, darling, but . . . Why do you suppose I've taken so long? I've been thinking. I tried to find a way, but there is no other way out. This is best."

"What is best?" he asked in horror.

"That I go with my people." Virginia moved to the table Martin had moved to the other end of the room. She sat down there, putting her hands before her on the table and examining them with disinterest.

Martin could only stand in the center of the room.

"Toby was right, Martin. I was born a Capellan. When I went back I saw my father. My mother. Bobby. I talked to them all. At first I was still filled with the desire to go against them all, but I see now I was wrong. You have your people. I have mine."

She shrugged resignedly. "I learned something else, too. When the Capellans leave they will take with them the device for creating the waves that energize the brain cells of men—those words hardly described how your reasoning power is maintained. But when it is taken away you must go back at once to only a few thousand years from where we found you. It will be chaos.

"I thought I might somehow prevent that from happening to you. I didn't want you to revert to a primitive thing, a mere hulk of a man who remembered so little of what he once knew. I could not stand it, Martin. But I have learned I cannot supply the force I thought I could. You would go back with everyone else."

Martin looked away. "I see."

"And as for me," she said bitterly, "I am an immortal. It would be my lot to live on Earth forever—alone, after they left. I would see, through the millions of years, the advancement of your race once again. I might conceivably help it, if it proved to be the dominant species, but even the power of a single Capellan is limited. That way I would not be fulfilling my destiny. It is with my people, as I have said. It is perhaps on some other star somewhere with another Capellan, to start a new colonization, if it is so decided."

She continued to look at her hands.

"Another thing," she said in a voice he could hardly hear. "They are leaving soon. There would be so little time . . ."

Martin moved to her. She looked up at him without expression. He lifted her from the chair, made her stand and face him.

He took her in his arms, kissed her savagely.

She did not resist.

When she did not respond, he knew she was telling the truth and he let her go and she dropped into the chair again.

"That's how it is . . . ?"

"That's how it is."

He went to a window he had recently cleaned. He looked out. He saw nothing.

"This is good-bye, then?"

"Yes. I'm sorry, Martin. If you only knew how sorry!"

He said nothing.

After a while he felt a cold breeze.

He shuddered.

He had stood at the window he did not know how long before he moved. His muscles ached with the effort. He would have liked to stand there forever, for life had suddenly become distasteful. But he knew he could not stand there any longer. He would have to face reality sooner or later.

When he turned he saw the table.

That is where she sat, he thought, just a few minutes ago.

Oh, God, let's not get elegiac about this. What's done's done. What do they say? Life must go on. Well, let it. But still, that is where she last sat, where she would not look at me but just kept looking at her hands.

He saw something at that moment he hadn't seen before. The gleam of metal where her hands had rested on the rough, hewn table.

It was a cube, a polished golden cube with a jewel in each face. It was just about the size of a cube of sugar.

He picked it up.

Instantly he felt her presence. In his mind's eye he could see her before him as he held the cube. She was beautiful, radiant, as she looked at him.

"Do not reveal the secret of the cube," she said with urgency. "They may still be watching you."

She smiled. "Martin, what I told you is not true. I do not want to go with my people, but I had to say so. They wanted to kill you because they think you are stopping me from going cheerfully with them.

"I promised to leave when they do. The price? Your life will be spared. But darling, I had a mental reservation. I will go only if I'm unable to reach you again."

Her eyes were wistful.

"Leave Tessie Valley, darling. Leave it as if you are sad. Go back to Chicago or wherever you would go. I will join you as soon as I can. I love you. Pray for my success."

She put her fingers to her lips, blew him a kiss. Then her image was gone.

The cube dissolved in his hand.

# 15

Local news traveled fast in the *National Scene* building. For example, if the girl behind the tobacco counter on the lobby floor were to come to work some morning with a ring on her third finger, left hand, it would not take more than an hour for this information to traverse the length, breadth and height of the office building.

Hands would pause for a moment on typewriter keys as it would be received; a few minutes later it might be relayed to others at the water cooler, an ever-widening circle of the informed.

The speed of transmission depended on the item.

National news, although it was the marketable commodity of all who were employed there, was relegated to an unimportant place in the immediate scheme of things, for national news happens every day; part of an ever-changing pattern that somehow always resembles the previous day's pattern. Therefore, it never seemed wholly new.

It came into the building in a number of ways. In a brief case carried by an associate editor, by private telephone, by Western Union, by telephone and, on rare occasions, such as on this day, in person.

Most of the workers there failed to become emotionally aroused by the news; they soon became inured to the perpetual chaos of domestic affairs that made their pay checks possible. Most left the thrill of it to the handlers of the news and even the majority of these people were disenchanted with it. Only the inner circle—the men in the editorial offices—got excited about it once in a while.

When Martin Enders walked into the *National Scene* building one dull morning in early November, the local news passers had his arrival up and down the building before he even stepped into the elevator.

(He walked off the job and ran away with this girl, see? Boy, his bosses were mad! Old Wilson didn't say much to anybody else, but I heard New York really poured it on him. Got that in the Teletype room. They say she's a blonde. Cute, too. Daughter of the guy he was interviewing for a story. The old duffer died of a heart attack right afterward, her father was so upset. He's got a lot of nerve walking in here just as if nothing happened!)

The elevator rose swiftly toward the eleventh floor.

An operator in the Teletype room hung up the phone, seated himself at a machine, set a piece of paper he had scribbled a few notes on under the clip and started to punch the keys.

URGENT: NEW YORK. NOTIFY MAJOR GENERAL WALTER DEEMS AS PER HIS INSTRUCTIONS THAT MARTIN ENDERS JUST WALKED IN CHICAGO OFFICE. WILL VERIFY AND EXPEDITE IF TRUE. WILSON.

When he emerged from the elevator on the eleventh floor editorial offices, he found every eye focused on him. Even Lovett Wilson's cigar glowed brightly in the doorway of his office as he stood there to verify what he had heard.

All action ceased as Martin stood momentarily in front of the closing doors of the elevators. Then he moved through the swinging gate and down the aisle between the desks. He had expected some comment, but no one ventured a word. He came to the managing editor's office.

"Come in, come in," Wilson said, stepping back and indicating a chair near his desk. As Martin passed him, Wilson poked his head outside the door and Martin heard Wilson say, "It's O.K. Get Myers."

Wilson looked him over carefully and said, "Where in hell have you been, Martin? Here, let me have your coat." He helped him off with it and hung it on a tree. He then went around to the rear of his desk. "We've been worried about you."

"It's a long story," Martin said.

URGENT: NEW YORK. NOTIFY DEEMS IT IS ENDERS. WE AWAIT HIS INSTRUCTIONS. WILSON.

Senior Editor Denton Myers strode in, stopped still in the doorway. "I can't believe it." He closed the door behind him. "For God's sake, whatever happened to you? Where did you disappear to?" He moved to a leather chair beside the desk facing Martin.

Martin sensed an unfathomable coolness about them, a certain wariness that made him uneasy. Something was up.

"Is it true about that girl?" Wilson asked. "Did you really run away with her?"

"Yes," Myers put in. "And what about that business with the ambulance?"

"You know about that?"

The men nodded.

"Whatever possessed you just suddenly to pull up stakes and take off, Martin? It's unlike you. You settled down pretty well after the army. You were one of the best men we had."

"As I said, Willie, it's a long story."

"Then the old man dying. His son died of pneumonia, too, a few days after that. Did you know that? Where is his daughter, the girl you're supposed to have run away with?" Wilson rolled the cigar around in his mouth.

"I just don't understand you, Martin," Myers said. "I couldn't believe it when they told me. You seemed so—so stable."

"Just what did you hear about me?" Martin asked.

"The first we knew, Colonel Sherrington was calling us. The story he told was that you ran off with the professor's daughter in one of the field ambulances."

"The colonel was pretty peeved," Myers said. "He ranted and raved all over the place. They blame you for Dr. Penn's death. They say the shock of your eloping with his daughter was just too much for his heart."

"Lucky for us," Wilson said, "we argued them out of preferring charges. When it looked like a simple love affair, Colonel Sherrington agreed to wink his eyes at it. But he'll never forgive you for what you did to the two soldiers. He broke them to privates."

"Really?" Martin was amused.

"What did you ever do to get them to tell that fantastic story about two walls?" Wilson's cigar had gone out and he lit it again. "They wouldn't get off it. They said you manufactured a wall and when they got out to investigate, you ran away in the ambulance. It was a stupid lie."

"Then there was the fire," Myers said. "The fire in the gatehouse. How did you manage that?"

"Was it a love affair?" Wilson asked, cocking an eye at him. "You can tell us. We'll keep it quiet."

"It was, in a way."

"Well, thank God for that," Myers said, letting out his breath in a long sigh. "There are some who have taken a dark view of what you've done. But of course that doesn't excuse you for not reporting to us. The least you might have done is let us know where you were."

"Myers is right, Martin," Wilson said. "We would not have liked it, but if you felt it was so damned important, we might have let you go on your spree with our blessings."

URGENT: CHICAGO. DEEMS WANTS YOU TO HOLD HIM

THERE IF YOU CAN BUT DO NOT USE FORCE. HE WILL BE FOLLOWED IF HE INSISTS ON LEAVING YOUR PLACE. TRY TO HOLD HIM TILL THEY GET THERE ANYWAY. CUMMINGS.

"You still haven't said anything," Myers said.

"You haven't given me a chance."

"Is the girl with you?"

Martin shook his head. "No. She isn't with me."

"Martin hasn't even said he ran away with her yet, Myers," Wilson said. "How about it?"

"I don't even know why I came here," he said. Could he tell them he came there because it would have been the natural thing to have done after Virginia left him in Utah? "The way things stand, you are worrying over something quite insignificant."

"Now what do you mean by that?" Lovett Wilson champed down hard on his cigar. Myers blinked his eyes. "If you think we're taking that little escapade of yours lightly——"

The phone rang.

"Pardon me." Wilson picked up the phone. The man in the teletype room read him the message from New York. "Thanks," Wilson said. He put the phone back.

Martin lit a cigarette and knew the telephone call had been about himself. There was a little more tension now in Wilson. Even Myers seemed to sense it; Martin fancied Myers wanted to ask Wilson what he had learned on the phone.

Something was up, all right.

"Why don't you go back to the beginning and tell us all about it?" Wilson suggested.

"You wouldn't believe me if I told you," he said. "You'd have me taken away in a strait jacket. It so happens I don't want to be put away."

The managing editor leaned forward across the desk. "We have a right to know, don't you think? After all, we've never taken you off the payroll."

"Martin, for heaven's sake, quit trying to be mysterious," Myers said impatiently. "If it's crazy, let us decide that."

Martin chuckled. "Well . . . What would you say if I said mankind is doomed?"

Wilson snorted, knocking an inch of ash off his cigar. "Hell, everybody knows that. Just wait till the H-Bomb falls." He brushed his suit coat where the ash had fallen.

"Or they dust the upper atmosphere with plague bacteria."

"You ought to see what we have in our files we can't put in the magazine," Wilson said. "Strictly from horror."

"Is it along that line?" Myers queried.

"No," Martin said. "I'll tell you, but you won't understand.

Man is shortly going to lose the reasoning power he possesses."

Wilson's cigar went limp in the center of his half-opened mouth and he looked at Martin with wonder. Then he glanced at Myers, the look was returned, and then he faced Martin again.

"Would you mind telling us, Martin, just how this is going to happen?"

"Because creatures from a planet circling Capella—Alpha Aurigae—will soon return there, taking with them the device that gave us reasoning power about fifty-thousand years ago, lifting us quickly above other species."

The two editors sat silent, self-forgotten.

"I see," Wilson finally said in a flat voice.

Denton Myers cleared his throat embarrassedly. "I suppose you have been, ah, trying to prevent this from happening. Is that it?"

"That's impossible."

"Is it?"

"Yes."

"You mean to say we can't stop this from happening?"

"Yes."

"Why?"

"Because they are invisible to us. They live on another plane."

"I see." Wilson tried to say it this time with conviction.

"I told you you wouldn't believe me."

"No," Wilson said, as if he were weighing the matter. "I wouldn't go so far as to say that. But you—would you mind telling us where the girl fits into this?"

"Yes. Tell us about the girl."

"She's a Capellan."

"I thought you said they were invisible. A lot of people have seen her."

"She hasn't gone back yet."

"Back . . . ?"

"To their plane. It's coexistent with this one. Many of them existed as human beings and Capellans simultaneously, going back for brief periods whenever they wished. Now they're all leaving by dying as humans, transferring to their plane."

Wilson made a steeple with his hands, pressed the forefingers to his lips and rocked in his office chair.

"I'll tell you what," he said. "Let me ring for my secretary. I want you to tell her all about it. Everything you can remember. You can use this office. Myers and I will stay here with you and hear all about it at the same time. We'd like to have this down in black and white."

Martin sensed another reason in the request and shook his head. He got to his feet. "Sorry," he said. "It is too fresh in my mind right now. I don't want to think about it."

Wilson came around the desk. "Well, if you don't like that idea, how about sitting out there at your desk and writing it up for us? Just how it happened. Don't leave anything out. Put it all in your usual, clear style. What do you say?"

"No." Martin took his coat from the clothes tree, but Wilson took it gently away from him.

"Now look, Martin. You've just come through what must have been a trying experience. We'd like to hear about it. Really we would. Think of the questions you've left unanswered! Why, people everywhere would want to hear about these—these——"

"Capellans," Martin said drily.

"Yes. We want something concrete. You hold the key to the whole thing. You say it is impossible to combat them. How do we know that's true? If you wrote it down or talked to us about it one of us might come up with the right idea. Myers, why don't you send out for a few drinks? Are you hungry, Martin? We could have a bite here. I'm starved, myself."

Martin smiled and took his coat. As he did so, Wilson's desperation engulfed him like muggy air. "What kind of funny business is going on, Willie? What did you hear on the phone?"

Wilson winced visibly. "It was nothing. Just a—an appointment that failed to show up. Had the flu, the man said. But to get back to you . . ."

Martin had his coat now. "I'm not buying it, Willie. I have a good idea of what you and Myers think of what I had to say."

"Now, Martin," Myers soothed.

"We believe you, don't we, Myers?" Wilson said. "We have no reason to think you're fabricating anything. Why, after all these years—sure, it's a little fantastic, but——"

"Too fantastic," Martin said. "Much too fantastic to try to relate. I'll be seeing you, gentlemen."

He left the office.

Perhaps it was a mistake to go back, he thought as he got into the elevator and made room for the man who followed him in. But I think that is what I would have done anyway. If I am to act as if it's all over between Virginia and myself, this makes as good sense as anything.

The continuous stare of the man in the car with him made him take notice of him. The man seemed to be trying to memorize his face. There was curiosity there; his mind reeked of purpose. He had been right. Something was up. This was it.

When Martin got into a cab, he saw the same man get into another. When Martin's cab was moving up Michigan Avenue to his apartment hotel, the Welmerly, he saw that there were two cabs following him now.

He did not worry about them. He had worried on the long trip to Chicago from Utah until he realized it would make no difference one way or the other if someone recognized him and turned him in. They probably wanted him, all right. He fancied there had been quite a furor when he and Virginia rushed out of Park Hill in the stolen ambulance; it surprised him to learn that Colonel Sherrington had preferred no charges.

He looked back. The cabs were still there. The three of them made an unhurried procession up the wide street.

He wondered what would happen if he should stop his cab and go back and tell the two shadows that their world was going to end soon.

"Look," he could say. "You're going back, fellows, back where you came from. You'll have long beards before long and maybe you'll pick up a club somewhere, if you have enough brains left to realize you need one."

It wouldn't be any use. They wouldn't believe him.

In his apartment he found a bottle he had left there and mixed himself a drink. He drank it in front of the window that overlooked the avenue from his third-floor apartment. He felt like shouting to the people rushing about in cars, to the woman walking her dog, to the young couple arm in arm, to his two shadows down there somewhere.

"Here's a toast to you all," he said, raising his glass. "To your ignorance of what's in store for you. Or maybe I should try to tell you. Awake and take stock, you people! Behold your reward: years of darkness!" No, that sounded too much like "Workers, arise!" Hell, they'd think I was a damned Commie, spouting stuff like that. Best I leave them alone.

He read again the letters on the dining-area table. He had opened them the previous night when he had arrived from the West. Bills. A few notes from friends. They were meaningless now.

It was nearly noon when he left the building for his lunch. The two men who had been following him appeared from nowhere and entered a near-by restaurant behind him. One of them took a table near his, obviously to overhear the conversation he might have with someone—if he were to meet someone there. You're on the wrong track, fella. The other man took a table near the door.

Back again at the apartment he settled down on the sofa-bed with a book, tried to get interested in it. He was awakened from a sound sleep by thunderous knocks on his apartment door.

He knew who it was before he opened the door.

General Deems walked into the room, followed by an army captain. The two shadows stood in the doorway.

"Close the door, Smollet," the general said.

The captain closed it and stood there. The general strode around the room, eyes flicking over the envelopes, the bottle of whisky, the book Martin had been reading. He turned to Martin.

"Any way out of here other than that door?"

"The window," Martin said. "But it's a drop of three floors."

The general stopped in the middle of the room, legs wide apart, hands in his army coat, eyes level with Martin's.

"Get your notebook out, Smollet," he said vigorously. "Mr. Enders is going to tell us all about it."

Captain Smollet took off his coat and hat, put them on the sofa-bed, arranged his notebook on the dining-area table, poised his pencil expectantly over the blank sheet.

Martin had not moved from beside the door. He had merely folded his arms and watched the captain with some amusement.

"Now, Enders, where is the girl?"

"I don't know." It was the truth.

"Were you two in this together?" The general's burning stare bore into him.

"What do you mean by 'this,' General?"

"You know damned well what I mean by 'this.' " General Deems showed how much he had been hurt by pacing the room, gesturing wildly as he talked. "What kind of fools do you take us for? You drop your investigation and run away with this blonde girl. Where did that put us? And all that stuff you're handing out about the stars—Wilson and Myers told me about that. What's your angle?"

"I was telling the truth."

"Come off it, Enders," the general jeered. "Who are you kidding? Who is behind it all? Who got to you? How much did he pay you? And while you're at it, who thought up all this gobbledegook you're passing off in an effort to cover up?"

"You would be amusing, General, if you weren't so pathetic."

The general's color deepened perceptibly. His eyes whipped at Martin and the room took warmth from his anger.

"You are something pretty dirty, Martin Enders," he seethed. "Selling your own country down the river. Don't tell me, I know. One of these smart boys with all the answers who thinks he can play both sides to win, place and show. Like so many bright boys, you don't have a heart. Major premise, minor premise and conclusion and to hell with the human element. If people don't fit in your equations forget them——"

"Just a minute!" Martin felt sudden anger burning like bowel pain inside him, resentment flaring in his brain. He crossed to the sofa-bed and sat on it, lighting a cigarette with a hand that trembled. "You have me confused with something and someone else," he said. "I don't like talk like that. I served my country honorably and well; you said my record shows that."

"But why——"

Martin put up his hand. "Don't start it again, please. I'm at fault, I suppose, the way I've acted. But I want to tell you something: what I've had to say is true!"

"For God's sake!" The general took off his hat, sailed it across the room where it hit the wall, bounced back and rolled a few feet on the floor.

"Will you listen, General? *Will you?*"

The general plopped into a chair, ran a hand over his bald head, into the grey bristles over his neck.

"It's just as I said. The Capellans will leave Earth soon. When they do, we'll lose our reason. That's why it doesn't make any difference what you do or what I do. A man about to be hanged makes jokes about it to those within hearing to prove he isn't afraid, though he may be quaking inside. I am like that man."

"Maybe you have lost your reason," the general said, studying his face. He softened. "Perhaps they are right, Wilson and Myers. They think you've gone off the deep end. I guess you have."

"The insane," Martin said evenly, "are usually happy. I am not."

"Why didn't you call me from Park Hill or after you left it? If you had tried to explain it then . . ."

"If I had called you, the Capellans would have known where we were. I had run away with a Capellan, you see. Dr. Penn was a Capellan, too——"

"The Capellans, the Capellans! That's all you talk about. Where are these—these Capellans? Where do they live? Show me *one* Capellan and I'll believe you."

"They are on another plane," Martin explained patiently. "For that reason, they are invisible to us."

"Invisible, eh?" The general eyed him thoughtfully. "If you believe that, then you *are* nuts. But I don't think you are. The girl figures in this somewhere and you've got her hidden. She's probably the one we really want. Where is this Virginia Penn?"

"Somewhere between heaven and Earth," Martin said.

"Getting flippant again, eh, Enders?" The general came over, hands on hips, standing menacingly over him.

"He's not flippant, General. He's wrong. I'm not between heaven and Earth. I'm right here in this room."

"Virginia!" Martin jumped from the sofa-bed, almost upsetting the general. He looked around. Virginia was not there.

"Who was that?" The general's face was purple. "You've got a recording, Enders. Mighty funny."

"Mighty funny." The voice was Virginia's. She laughed.

"Where are you, Virginia?"

"You shut up," the general said. "Smollet!"

The captain, who had been trying to find the source of the voice himself, rose. "Yes, sir!"

"Give this room a thorough examination for that loud-speaker."

"Martin said Capellans are invisible," Virginia said. "So we are. You'll find no loud-speaker here."

Captain Smollet was looking in lamps, behind books, in corners, along the molding.

"It's no use, Captain Smollet," Virginia said. "You won't find anything."

Martin felt the gratifying rush of cold wind, saw Virginia materialize in a corner of the room.

"Here I am, General," she said, smiling sweetly.

# 16

"More of your tricks, Enders," the general said a little uncertainly. "Where have you been hiding her?"

"You are a mighty hard man to convince, aren't you, General?" Virginia said, moving toward him, smiling mischievously.

"Thank God you came back, Virginia," Martin said. "I thought you might not make it."

"You stay where you are, Miss Penn," the general said. "I don't know where you came from, but now that you're here, you can tell us why you and Mr. Enders ran away from Park Hill."

"I suggest you go home to your wife and children, General," Virginia said, seating herself next to Martin. "You'll find in a few days your question has no importance."

"Am I going to get double talk from you, too?"

Virginia fixed him with a fishy eye. "People usually find the truth hard to believe."

The flush of red which had momentarily receded was rising again in the general's face.

"I ought to run you both in," he said. "I ought to let you sit it out in separate cells in some cold, dank county jail while you are being investigated. But there's no time for that. I've got to know now. *Today!*"

"What is it that is really bothering you?"

The general put his hands to his forehead, ran the palms past his temples.

"What happened to Forrest Killian? Who is behind the move to stop the regeneration project? Why? And what part do you two have in this whole thing? Do you think you can answer that?"

"I'll answer them in order," Virginia said. "Forrest Killian is—dead, you would say. The molecules that composed his being have been scattered far and wide. No one at the present time is trying to stop regeneration; there is no need to. Martin and I have no place in it any longer. We merely want to be together to the end."

"The end? The end of what?"

"Your civilization."

The general threw his hands in the air. "I give up," he

said. "I've tried to be decent. I've tried to give you both a chance to be truthful, but you are evasive. Do you frankly expect anyone to believe this hogwash about losing reasoning power—this star business?"

"It really doesn't matter, General," she answered.

"It so happens that it does matter, young lady," he whipped back.

"Are you tired of this?" Virginia asked Martin, sitting up straight as if she were going to do something about it.

"Frankly, yes."

The general only glared at them.

Virginia sat very still, furrowed her forehead slightly in thought.

The general looked uncomfortable. Captain Smollet was frankly puzzled.

Then both their mouths dropped open in amazement. The general's arm rose and met with resistance. His fingers were running along something solid before him. He was speaking and Captain Smollet was answering, looking at something in wonder. But their voices were muffled and could hardly be heard.

"There," Virginia said, settling back. "That ought to keep them occupied for a while." She looked at Martin, who met her eyes with questioning ones of his own. She laughed. "You've heard of these one-way mirrors, haven't you? Well, I put one between us and the officers. We can see them and they can't see us. Cozy, don't you think?"

Martin watched the searching, feeling officers in their amazement. They had called in the two shadows who had been just outside the door. All four of them were running their hands along the air.

"Miss me?" Virginia cupped her hand behind his head.

"Damn right!" He drew her to him, kissed her soundly. "How much time do we have?"

"Departure Day is three days from now. Actually, I don't know when they'll stop sending out the thought-reinforcing radiations. Probably shortly before they leave Earth."

"You're going with them, I suppose?"

Virginia shook her head. "I waited until the last Capellan returned from his Earthly existence. Then I came back. In this way I knew I'd run into none of them here."

"They could be watching."

"Too busy getting ready to leave. Oh, they could appear, I suppose. But I don't think they will. Got a cigarette?"

He lit two. "You still haven't answered me. Are you going with them?"

She examined the lighted end of her cigarette. "No."

"But what you said back in Utah—I will turn into——"

"A cave man?" She smiled. "What's wrong with a cave man? You'd make a cute one. You'd look nice in a beard."

"But you don't want that!"

"You'd have no inhibitions . . ."

Her remark and her nearness stirred him, but he said, "You're making light of it. You know it won't be pretty."

"I will lose much of my power, too, I've learned," she said gravely. "There probably is nothing I could do to help you retain your intelligence. But"—and she was grim—"I've made my decision. I've found you and I'm going to stick by you."

He kissed her and held her head against his chest. "Promise me," he said, "promise me you'll go back—just before the end."

"They wouldn't have me now. They will find I'm gone and this time they'll forget about me. They'll think, Good riddance to bad rubbish. I've been too errant. Besides, I don't want them to see me again. They know I wouldn't go back with them even if they did come after me."

They jumped at a terrible pounding. One of the shadows had picked up a chair and was hammering the partition with it.

"Will it hold?"

"Yes. But that noise!"

There were more people on the other side now: a policeman, two men in work clothes and many faces out in the hallway. They were all talking to each other and each person had to come over to feel the partition and register astonishment.

"That's enough of that," Virginia said. "They'll have everybody and his brother out there soon. Let's see. There ought to be some way . . ."

"Not a fire again," Martin said.

"No. That would only bring more people. We've got to get them out of here."

"The only way to do that," Martin said glumly, "is for us to leave."

"That's it!" she cried, flashing him a smile.

"But we can't do that! I mean, we don't want to."

"Come on," she said, getting up from the sofa and drawing him to another part of the room next to the partition.

"First," she said, "we create us." She concentrated, narrowing her bright blue eyes and pouting her full red lips.

In a little while the air moved about in the area around the sofa, the light rippled and eddied and two shapeless masses were created there.

"I'm not much of a sculptress," she said. "Let me know if

I'm doing this wrong." She continued her concentration.

The shapeless masses suddenly took shape. There was the blonde hair, lovely, wavy blonde hair, the blue eyes—how they sparkled!—the curving form, the legs.

"That's not the same dress," Martin said. "And besides——"

"I know. The skirt is too short." She laughed. "They'll be so busy looking at my knees—I hope—they'll forget it's not the same outfit. Now don't go prudish on me and tell me it's not nice."

The man took shape. Martin Enders to a "T."

"You see," Virginia said. "I can't improve on you."

The two duplicates sat looking vacantly ahead. Little by little they came alive. Suddenly Martin's double took his Virginia in his arms and kissed her passionately.

"You see what my dress does to you?" Virginia said.

"My head is easily turned," Martin commented.

Virginia's double slapped her Martin. He looked amazed.

"Now, children," Virginia said. "You *are* brain children, you know."

The two on the sofa looked at her without surprise.

"I will create a door," Virginia said. "I want you two to go through it. Do whatever the general on the other side says. You are to go where he tells you, try to act as much like us as possible. I will be watching you. Is that clear?"

The two nodded. The other Martin held her hand.

"Isn't he sweet?" Virginia giggled.

"He probably resents that label."

"You're sweet," the other Virginia said.

"You're an angel," the other Martin said.

"See? He doesn't resent it. You never called me an angel."

Virginia was thoughtful once again. A crack appeared in the air and a silver doorknob materialized in the wall of nothing.

The two duplicates rose, the other Martin turned the doorknob, opened the door and they passed through. The door clicked shut behind them, the crack and the doorknob vanishing.

The people on the other side milled around the newly created couple. The general elbowed his way through, was gesturing and, from the looks of his throat muscles, was also quite vehement.

The crowd dispersed as soon as the other Martin and Virginia had been escorted out of the room.

"Well," Virginia said. "They're gone."

Martin looked at her sharply. She was tired. Though she still looked toward the door, there was not the look of triumph on her face he expected. Her shoulders sagged and he noticed for the first time the dark circles under her eyes.

He had sensed inner conflict; the hysterical quality of her return, her delight with the mirror-wall and the creation of the other couple attested to a temporary escape from a problem. He could feel the residual tenseness in her.

"Why so glum all of a sudden?"

"Was I glum?" she said, brightening. "I didn't mean to be. I was merely thinking how ironical it is that now we have found ourselves, there is a time limit."

"Why do your people have to take along this device you mention which affects our higher thinking? If they would only leave it, there would be no problem."

"The original Three—the mother, father and their first son —look on Earth's present civilization as an artificial thing, a state they created," Virginia explained. "As someone would do who visited, they are to leave this planet much as they found it. I have been told it is always done that way."

"You mean this has been done before?"

"Many times before on other worlds, according to our history, but of course not by the group here now. The original couple came from a planet such as yours. That other planet was made to revert back to its crude beginnings when the group left it to go back to Capella Four. You see, there is a limit to the amount of progress allowed. You have reached that point. You would have either advanced fast to the next step, or you would have destroyed yourselves. We might have profited from the latter; the Triumvirate feels it would be dangerous to allow the former."

"Why not leave and just let us advance? I still don't see why not."

"You have grown too fast," Virginia said. "You have too many primitive tendencies. You have advanced fast technologically while you have stood still for many hundreds of years sociologically. If left as you are, there would be none of us around to curtail your warlike natures. You are not a very model society by our standards. If you had advanced this far in millions of years, you would have lost many of these bad traits during the process. But you haven't. You have done it overnight—with our help. To put it bluntly, you are too close to the savage."

"Is that what you see in me, Virginia?"

"Not at all," she said gently. "There is an unknown quality about your mind that I enjoy. You are not like other men I've known. And as long as I'm being frank, I'll say there's something about you that makes my heart skip a beat when you come into the room. Love?" She nodded. "My people say

I am mad. I am so—about you. Else why should I be here?"

Suddenly there was a look of alarm in her eyes. They had been fixed on Martin, but now they were looking at something beyond him, far distant. She sat up straight.

"What is it?"

"I thought they were through with me," she said with concern. "Now I feel them searching—I can sense their probing minds." Now she got to her feet, put her hands to her cheeks. "Why can't they let me be!"

The full force of discouragement strangled Martin's will. If they were seeking Virginia, if there were more than one, then this must be the end, for she had made a promise to them and she had not kept it. They would be vengeful and all-powerful and what could he hope to do in the face of their wrath? Her consternation was only evidence of her inability to combat those of her own kind.

Virginia sank beside him and she looked so dismayed he pressed her to him and comforted her.

"Let them come," he said. "Perhaps it is better this way."

Then she broke away. "No! They know I am here because of that mirror-wall I made and the telltale emanations accompanying the creation of the other you and me. Let me see." She studied the air. "The other two of us are now downtown. We are walking from a car to an entrance to a building. *Run!* We are running away. We are coming to a corner. There is shooting, but it does not matter. There! We've rounded a corner." She turned to him. "We've just vanished. Now that's done. Let's get out of here!"

He answered the urgency of her voice. "Now that you've stopped radiating anything, why must we leave here?"

"They'll probably zero in here. We don't want to be here when they do."

Together they started for the door. Martin approached the spot where the invisible wall had been, put his foot gingerly forward but met no obstacle.

"Come on," she said. "That's been gone a long time."

At the open door she collided with an invisible barrier, gave a cry and whirled, white-eyed.

Dr. Eric Penn stood in the middle of the room.

The enormous man's eyes were intent, his mouth was devoid of humor; there was an aura of authority and decision about him. Gone were his glasses, his ever-present pipe. His arms hung at his sides and his long fingers were whiter than they had been the last time Martin had seen him. He was clad in a dark suit, white shirt and blue tie; there was a handkerchief peeping out of his breast pocket.

Martin wondered if it was the suit he had been buried in.

"You little fool!" he said sharply. "They're all laughing at you."

"Let them laugh!" Virginia flung back.

"I don't know what they'll do to you now. But I know what I ought to do. The Earth people have a habit of spanking their children. I can see its application for the first time."

Virginia's eyes flashed. "That is what I don't like about all of you. You are treating me as a child. You are all cast in the same mold, all doing the same things over and over—never a deviation. Suddenly someone does something a little different . . ."

"Why did you have to do it, Virginia? My own daughter!"

Virginia went up to him. "You are my father and I love you very much. But I also happen to love Martin. Can't any of you see that?"

"But don't you know the folly of it? If we were staying, I'd say see it through. But we're leaving. We can't leave you here like this. Besides, you have disobeyed."

She spun around. "I don't care."

"I have been sent to bring you back."

"I won't go." She came to Martin and he put an arm around her; they both stared defiantly at her father.

"There are ways," her father said.

"Martin and I *both* die, then."

"You know that's impossible."

"If you kill him"—Virginia drew in her breath—"I'll—I'll—"

Dr. Penn looked at her despairingly.

"I don't understand you, Virginia." He shook his head resignedly. "You failed to keep your promise to us and as far as I know, it's the first time you've ever done that. Why are you causing so much trouble for us now when we are so near leaving? Is it really because of him?"

When Virginia did not answer, Dr. Penn turned to Martin as if seeing him for the first time. "Mr. Enders," he said. "You are responsible for something that has never happened before in Capellan history: one of us has fallen in love with someone of Earth—and, I suppose, vice versa. You love Virginia, I suppose?"

Martin nodded.

"What do *you* suggest we do about it?"

"Me?" Martin smiled ruefully. "This is the first time my opinion has been solicited when there have been Capellans about. I find it a rare experience."

"Yes, I know," Dr. Penn said drily. "Maybe I am clutching at straws, but I've heard about you. Virginia would talk of nothing else. But come, surely you have a suggestion."

"In order to have a suggestion for a way out of difficulty, there must first be a difficulty," Martin said. "I fail to see one here."

"No problem?" Dr. Penn eyed him warily. "You mean we ought to let Virginia stay and not go back with her own people?"

"Certainly," Martin said. "Why not? Just because she's doing something no one else among you ever thought of doing, why not let her do it? Why try to understand it?"

"But we can't leave her behind!"

"Why not?"

"Why not! It's unthinkable. She'd be living here forever. In the remembrance of time immemorial, Martin Enders will have been but the merest fraction of her full memory. Why should she throw her whole future away just for a few minutes with you? There are those of her own kind she could be with forever."

"Don't you suppose she's thought of that?" Virginia's hand found Martin's arm and the fingers tightened to indicate she agreed.

"All right," Dr. Penn said. "All right. I have been authorized to make one other offer." He took Virginia's hands in his and she did not stop him. "Will you return, Virginia, if we take Martin along and see what we can do about taking him with us to Capella Four?"

She snapped alert at that. "Oh, Dad, do you think they might do that?"

"It looks as if that's the only way out." He turned his back on Martin and before long, forms materialized before him. Faces first, then bodies, appendages, hands, legs. People. There were first a few, then many eyes focused on him. When there became too many faces to count, Dr. Penn turned to Martin.

"It is understood, Mr. Enders, that you are something more than an average man. As such, you are asked to co-operate with us." He indicated the people behind him with a sweep of his arm. "These Capellans appear here to lend credence and psychological weight to what we shall try to do."

When Dr. Penn paused, Martin could feel his brain being searched by probing fingers of many minds.

"Do you want to go with us?"

The idea had started as a hard, undigested lump in his brain; it was something he had not thought of before. Now, as his mind sought it out and considered it, the meaning of it unsteadied him. *To leave Earth!* His mind reeled . . .

"I don't know," he replied honestly. "I never thought I'd have the choice."

"Perhaps you'd better wait until we find out whether or not it is possible," Dr. Penn said. "Now . . . We shall try something, Martin. Just leave your mind blank for a while. You will feel a surge of power. If you are what Virginia says you are, a better than average man, you ought to be able to attach yourself to this force and hold it, riding it as one would a dangling rope. Are you ready?"

Martin nodded. "Yes."

"Now . . ."

The faces concentrated—the eyes of Dr. Penn blazed with power—then the sides of Martin's head fell inward and there was a mighty rush of force immediately following the implosion—the faces grew whiter, sharper, brighter, turning into light, whirling, scintillating forms.

Suddenly he was aware of Virginia's fingernails digging hard into the hand she was holding.

Then there was nothing.

# 17

"Can you see?"

It was not a voice, but it was a query. A question that came out of the void and impinged itself somewhere in the nerve patterns of his brain and demanded an answer.

He said, "No." Though he had worked his tongue against the roof of his mouth, the word did not emanate from his mouth and he did not hear it within himself.

"He can't see."

"This is difficult."

"Are you sure he can make it?"

"Who can say? It's never been tried before."

"Perhaps he doesn't have enough mentality."

*"He does!"*

Martin smiled. That was Virginia. The thought that she was somewhere out there made him feel better.

The blackness changed; it was as if someone backstage had thrown the master switch—slowly. It grew light. He could see now for an infinite distance, but there was nothing to see. He looked down but he could not see his own body. This unsteadied him.

"What do you see now?"

"Light." He heard his own uttered word this time.

"That's better."

"Can you see us?"

He looked around. "No."

"He's coming along. We've restored his medium of communication by voice, but he did understand the mental questions. Did you notice that?"

"Of course he did." It was Virginia again. "I told you he would."

"Yes, but he cannot see us."

Silence. Then there were broken areas of grey and these brightened to orange blobs of light.

"Do you see us now?"

"Yes," he said, watching the dancing wisps of color. "But you are like flames."

The light flickered momentarily, then it steadied. The irregular shapes of orange became human pink and there were sharper lines of definition. He looked down at himself, saw his arms and legs and felt whole once again.

When he looked up, he saw people standing as he was on a white plane that stretched endlessly in every direction to the horizon where the effulgent sky began and illuminated the scene with a soft glow. It reminded him of a painting by Dali; the only thing missing was a floppy watch. The people were common, ordinary-looking Earth people clad as any random group on Earth would have been. They were all men and they were looking at him.

"We have given you something to stand on." The voice came from beside him and he found Dr. Penn there, smiling at him. "You couldn't see in our area; we have made ourselves visible and you see shapes you can comprehend."

He felt a hand in his; Virginia was at his other side.

Now the men before him were taking seats behind a long table that had not been there a moment before.

"Shall we sit down?"

Dr. Penn indicated an upholstered bench that had materialized behind them and the three sat on it.

Martin studied the men before him. Judiciously placed in the center of the table sat a fat man with slick black hair and small, close-set eyes. He was talking to a white-haired man next to him. Others at the table were talking to each other, glancing at him once in a while. It was unnerving, this being talked about. Martin could not hear the whispered comments and he was about to ask Dr. Penn what was happening when the fat man rose.

"Dr. Penn," the slick-haired one said. "We have formed here as you suggested. Will you reiterate the problem, please?"

"Brother Capellans," Dr. Penn said, getting to his feet. "As you all probably know, my daughter, Virginia, refuses to leave Earth without the Earth-man, Martin Enders, whom we have advanced momentarily to this area. I realize it is not in order, especially with everyone preparing to depart this planet, but I have requested this session of a volunteer summary judicial committee to earnestly consider his transformation."

They all looked at Martin as the doctor sat down. Some were curious, some were cold. Others were amused.

"Mr. Enders." It was the fat man again. "I am Klell. I was among the last of the Capellans to leave my Earthly home—a body similar to yours. I might add that I'm glad of it."

Those at the table laughed politely and he acknowledged this with a slight bow to both sides.

"All of us here once lived on Earth," he said. "We were

encased in an inhibiting multicellular body most of the time, thankfully able to escape it for a little while when we visited among people of our own kind on our own level. Before my demise, I happened to be the owner of a gas station, though my activities, you understand, were not limited to pumping gasoline into people's cars."

More laughter. Martin supposed it was a remark calculated to refer, in a snide way, to the Capellans' real purpose on Earth.

"I think this whole thing is ridiculous." A young man at the extreme right of the table was the speaker. "I volunteered for this session because I don't think any of us wants one of *them* among us."

"Couldn't you stand the competition, François?"

The dark youngster flashed black eyes at Virginia, set his jaw firmly and looked back at Klell. "It is only a bid for attention by Virginia Penn."

A blond, sun-tanned and athletic fellow a head taller than the others, rose from the other end of the table. "I agree with François Chartres," he said. "This hearing *is* ridiculous. The fact that Virginia Penn wants this Earth-man is only further proof of the nature of her whims and caprices."

"Gentlemen!" Klell smiled at Martin. "Perhaps I ought to explain, Mr. Enders. François and Clarence Cavanaugh have—how shall I say it?—prior rights to Virginia."

"I disclaim that," Virginia said. "I have told them how I feel. They are merely giving voice to the well-known Earth habit of sour grapes. I tried to find love in me for them, but there was none."

"How can you possibly love an Earth-man, Virginia?" François looked hurt. "What can he give you that we cannot? Don't you remember our carefree days in school?"

"I certainly do," Virginia retorted coldly. "As I remember, you were always lazy and dissatisfied with yourself, content to let your Capellan superiority carry you through."

"You couldn't say that about me," Clarence said. "You remember? You said when you found me you couldn't understand how a man of François's caliber could have interested you. If I may say so, I think you told me François reminded you of an Earth cow the way he chewed gum."

Virginia turned to him. "You weren't much better, Clarence. Given an opportunity to be Capellans on Earth, you were both born to a heritage neither of you deserved. Your worst habit, Clarence, was wearing the most garish clothes to draw attention to your cultivated sun-tan. What would you have been as a pure Capellan? You were proud of something which had been merely provided through genetic engineering—the same thing that exists where you sit right at this moment, the replica of your attractive Earth body."

The laughter had been growing as the conversation had gone along and it spilled over into general guffaws up and down the line at this point. It even amused Martin, though he had thought Capellans would be above such humor.

"Actually, that is beside the point," Klell said. "If Mr. Enders were to come along with us he would find Virginia as capricious as the rest of us have found her. What would happen if she were to find someone else? But no matter, the decision as to whether or not we shall permit Mr. Enders to accompany us has not been made yet.

"Now, Mr. Enders, suppose we do take you along?" Klell leaned forward to study him better. "What about your heredity? Don't you realize it would be a millstone around your neck? How do we know you won't regress? How could you be a Capellan with such a recent primitive history?"

"Must we listen to all this?" It was François. "Let's have the vote."

"If you will please be quiet," Klell said. "How can we expect something like Martin to understand anything unless we write it out for him?"

"You're wasting our time," Cavanaugh said.

Virginia's fingernails were biting into Martin's arm. He looked at her and saw that her eyes mirrored the anger he was beginning to feel. They had no intention of taking him along—or had they? Could it be a test?

"You and other Earth people like you, Martin Enders, have tried to dominate your environment," Klell was saying. "What have you done? What progress have you made? You have failed because your lower, baser instincts still dominate you."

"How could we progress when you stood in our way?" Martin replied. "What chance did we have when you threw us into war after war?" He was surprised at his own vehemence and amazed at the response. Heads jerked around like puppet heads and eyes examined him with renewed interest. There was an accompanying titter of laughter.

Klell pointed a fat finger at him. "That is proof of it right there! The giving vent to rage without a considered opinion!"

Dr. Penn cleared his throat. "I don't think his statement could be attributed to anger, Klell."

"You cannot enter the discussion, Eric," Klell said coldly. "To answer Mr. Enders, however, I would have him look at the record: if it were not for the wars we caused, it is doubtful humanity would have progressed at all. His historians tell us wars and man's intense interest in new ways to slaughter those of his own kind has created machines which help and improve his lot in times of peace."

Suddenly Virginia's fingers drew blood.

"Why are you doing this to him?" she cried, tears starting. "You know what he is. You know men. You've lived among them."

"Yes, we know," Klell said gravely. Heads nodded.

"Then why?"

"Do you really want to know?" Klell looked at her seriously. "Very well. We've had enough humor, now let us proceed to the real reasons. In the beginning there was equilibrium among all living things on this planet. There was no reason for the worms and other early living organisms to change.

"Take the lowly sandworm, for there were sandworms on Earth then as there are now. They had even then subsisted for millions of years, these sandworms. Then one day a sandworm was born which was just a little less adapted than the others. That was the best sandworm. Why? It had to change in order to adapt itself. It was, shall I say, not so perfect as a worm, but more perfect in that it led the way for others to follow."

Klell's eyes looked far away. The people at the table were silent.

"You have come a long way, Sandworm Enders. Only you're a sandworm no longer. Now you have intelligence. An intelligence created and sustained by our thought reinforcer.

"You're a blind man to us, Mr. Enders. Among us you move as a blind man would move among your own kind, tapping your white cane. As you help the blind, so we've helped you, only you've insisted on going in wrong directions. Let us say you have endeavored as a civilization, but you have struggled in the quagmire of your own stupidity all along the way. You see, to us you are but a struggling subpersonality. Why should we take on the task of transforming a single such unworthy creature?"

Klell's statements made Martin feel microscopically small. Of course the human race was nowhere near the Capellan, but why did he have to rub it in?

"If you please," Martin said. "I wasn't begging——"

"Your conception of the universe," Klell swept on, "is founded on your inadequate senses. Why, you are not aware of the merest fraction of all the vibrations surrounding you. What part of the spectrum can you see? There are radiations visible to us which go through your brain without leaving a trace in your consciousness. Why should we make you any better than you are?

"And what, after all, do you know of life? Can you tell us what makes a group of molecules suddenly surge with power and come alive? Do you have any idea of what gravitation is? Of course not.

"You are still that lurking, skulking anthropoid found by the first two Capellans when they landed on this planet. Oh, you have intelligence now, but you won't have it when we remove the crutch you have used since we first arrived."

Klell stood proudly, his head high, looking down disdainfully at Martin as if daring him to say something.

"I suppose you think it's unanswerable, all this you've said," Martin snapped. "You forget the intelligence you have given us has also given us shame, a moral sense and a sense of remorse. These are indicative of evolutionary progress."

"Progress? You have retrogressed, Mr. Enders. Your sight isn't as good as it once was. Your sense of smell has become so impaired and your hearing has so declined that neither is adequate for survival. When we leave, other animals will make short work of you. It would be interesting to know which species will win.

"As for that intelligence, what have you done with it? Great men among you have tried to lead you upward. What have you done with them? You've killed them. You don't even trust each other, so you kill your own kind. And when you're not killing each other, you're killing yourselves in the machines you've invented. It is amusing how easy it has been for us to take advantage of your inhumanity to each other—even to yourselves!"

There was a ripple of applause along the table and Klell bowed to the right, then to the left.

"Friend Capellans, we have convened here to consider Capellan Penn's request for transformation for this man. I ask you, is this the kind of man we want to take along with us? A man whose genes contain the lust for blood, the greed, the latent savagery that could ripen and flower at any time? Do we want a human among us who could regress? Do you all share my feeling that Capellan Penn has wasted our time with this demand for a hearing?"

The faces at the table were thoughtful.

Martin could stand no more of it. He rose.

"I have listened to your indictment of the human race," he said levelly. "I want——"

"Of course you have," Klell said. "You were meant to hear it. But it so happens you are not the judge in this matter."

"I insist that I be heard!"

"Mr. Enders," Klell said. "We are quite aware of what

moves you. We've heard enough from you. Now if you will sit down, please, we will conduct the vote."

"I will not sit down," Martin said firmly. "Is this Capellan justice? Can no man say something in his own behalf?"

"Let him speak," someone said.

There were other voices in agreement.

"Very well." Klell sat down.

Virginia looked at Martin. There was admiration and hope in her eyes.

"You assume every one of us has a lust for blood, that everyone on Earth is greedy and that, in the breast of every man, there is a smoldering fire of latent savagery. How wrong you are! How little you have come to know men! There are many of us trying to free a world from its fetters of a primitive inheritance. Many of us devote and dedicate our lives to it.

"There are other words in our vocabulary besides the foul ones you mentioned, Mr. Klell. We have such words as generosity, kindness and brotherly love. Are these unfamiliar to you? Or have you forgotten words you might have once known, Mr. Klell? Is there by any chance a word for justice in Capellan speech?"

The Capellans were fidgeting, Martin noticed with satisfaction.

"Now you are going to leave us," Martin hurried on before anyone could interrupt. "Well, someday we would have emerged from our moral lethargy and we would have built a better world had you left us the seed to make this possible. But you are even denying us that, for you must remember it is you people who are at fault for making us move too fast for your own selfish gains. Yes, you are the selfish ones, pushing us this way and that, letting us suffer, rushing us along technologically without helping us along sociologically.

"And one more thing. Such a meeting as this would never be necessary in the United States where I come from. And another thing: There a man has a right to be heard."

"You were given permission to speak," Klell said hotly.

"Only because I demanded it."

"Yours is a very unusual case."

"All the more reason to weigh what I have said more carefully," Martin replied.

"Your speech is all very pretty," Klell said. "But we have been wasting time. We will take a vote now."

Martin stood very straight. He drew in his breath, let it out very slowly.

"There is no need to take a vote," he said. "I have made the decision for you. *I am not going with you.*"

Virginia uttered a cry, clutched at his arm.

"I have received enough Capellan beneficence," Martin said. "If the rest of humanity were to stand here beside me, I'm sure they would all feel the same way. You see, we have a little something called pride—we'll even admit we wouldn't have that if it hadn't been for you. But for your plans to take me along with you, I want none of it. I want to go back to the people I came from. I want to go back where I feel at home. I want to be stripped of my thinking and sent back along jungle paths, for I would rather be a primitive animal than take any more of your charity. You have used us long enough; now let us alone to grow the way we were supposed to in the first place."

"No!" It was Virginia who uttered the cry and she was beside him now, eyes welling with tears. She embraced him, held him.

Martin only stood defiant before the committee.

Suddenly they were gone.

# 18

Martin had supposed that he would be returned to his apartment on Michigan Avenue and that that would be the last he would ever see of the Capellans. Already, as the people vanished, he was conditioning himself for the shock of returning to his normal environment, trying to justify his actions.

He could not have been a true Capellan, he knew. He might have been one of them in spirit and in body, but he would also have been an Earth-man who had been transformed into a Capellan. What physiological and mental changes that might have meant he could only imagine. If he should have existed with them on Capella Four for all eternity, there would surely have come a time when it would have made a difference. And there might have come a time, too, when Virginia would have tired of him and would turn to one of her own kind. What of Martin Enders then?

He thought of the impending destruction of men's minds on Earth, the snuffing out of all they had learned—as if a blackboard filled with the facts of human history since the beginning of reason were to be erased. He also thought of his survival on a far distant world possessing the greater intelligence the Capellans would have implanted within him and he knew it was not the right thing to do. He had to admit it was an alluring and exciting prospect, but he had also to examine his own conscience. It was his conscience that stopped him. Now that the decision had been made, he was suddenly at peace with himself.

Earth is where I belong, he said to himself, fancying that he would materialize inside his apartment at any instant. It is where I was born and it is where I ought to die. I am of Earth and shall die of Earth.

Knowing he could be hurt no more, he turned his attention to the world in which he found himself. It was a beautiful, though chaotic, one. Apparently weightless and formless, he drifted through space as a dust mote would, rising, falling, caught by an eddy now and then and swinging around. Wherever he went there were blues, reds, purples, some harsh, others soft. There were colored giant cubes and spheres which changed into varied-hued rectangular solids of light as he swung into them; they were different on the inside: there were likely to be skies of brilliant stars or long vistas of velvet that disintegrated into dazzling streaks of light as he broke into them.

Some of the forms and shapes moved, others did not. It reminded him of the colors that sometimes swirled before his eyes when he was going to sleep. Though it was all weird, there was a pattern in it that soothed him. There was something he found in this kaleidoscopic world that put him at ease; there was force there, a force that seemed to be examining him, turning him this way and that.

Suddenly *she* was there. At his side. He could sense her but he could not see her.

"Why did you do it?" she asked in anguish. "Why won't you go along?"

"I love you, Virginia," he said. "But I could not go with you. I would always be an outsider. I see that now and I would see it in every eye."

"I know, darling, but I will always be an outsider, too. I have loved an Earth-man. Do you think they will ever forget that?"

"I suppose I have ruined your life," he said. "But you will forget me. You'll find someone else. You must not come with me."

"I'll never love anyone else and I can't come to live the final days with you now after all that's happened," she said sadly. "You might have gone with us."

"I'm sorry." It saddened him to know for certain she would not come. He had hoped she might. But he had spurned her people's offer, even before the vote. She was right; how could she pridefully throw away her life with her own people for a man who spoke as he did of them?

"Where am I now?" he asked. "Aren't they sending me back?"

"Yes," she said. "They are sending you back."

There was silence as he floated through worlds of color and design.

"If I am going back, why is it taking so long?"

"Perhaps they are waiting until just before we leave."

"How are you going to leave Earth? Do you have space ships?"

"It is only a step to Capella Four from here. In this dimension you are not hampered by distances as you are in yours."

"But what are these colors I see?"

"You are among Capellans. This is how they look to you on the plane you happen to be at the moment. They are all around you but they are paying you no attention and they are shunning me. I'm afraid I am a black sheep among them now."

Suddenly there was a crackling sound, the colors moved violently and Virginia uttered a hoarse cry.

Martin felt as if an elevator had dropped from beneath him. This must be it . . . Good-bye, Virginia.

*"Martin Enders!"*

It was a louder voice than he had ever heard before, yet it was not in the audible realm. It exploded inside his head in a brilliant show of colors.

There was a gasp. Virginia was still there.

The colors ceased their movement, then coalesced. His motion stopped. He had weight again and Virginia was at his side. They were in an enormous room lighted by glowing orbs set in the high ceiling and at the far end of the room a man sat, unmoving, in a large high-backed chair.

"Walk forward."

The voice was gentle, deep and resonant. There could be no thought of denying the command. As they walked toward the speaker, their steps echoed from the far walls, from the distant ceiling.

When they had reached a point twenty feet before him, the man held up his hand. They stopped.

The man was deceptively young in body, for behind the shining black pupils of his eyes there lurked the memory of centuries. His brown hair was coarse and fell back from his forehead in waves; his lean face was oval and his manner was firm.

"I am Myza, Mr. Enders. My wife and I were the first Capellans on Earth. She and I and our son, Prator, are what is called the Triumvirate. We are in charge of this Capellan colony.

"Although many of my people have, I have not lived on your Earth and taken human form through birth or even through the simple expedient of projecting myself since the original years. That has been the job of so many others of us —Virginia, for example, and other members of her family. In order to create the civilization necessary for a successful cultivation of our own kind, it was necessary to mingle with the Earth creatures and assume their shapes. This was done most unobtrusively through the birth process, as you probably know.

"I have taken this shape only because I presume this is what I would look like if you could see me through Capellan eyes. I was interested in your decision not to go with us to

Capella Four, now that our mission here has been successfully completed.

"I understand why. It was intended that you feel that way, for whether you guessed it or not, you could not have come along with us under any circumstances. We have no power to take anyone with us. The drama in which you took part was merely to teach you and Virginia how impossible it would be for you to live among our people, the doubts that would assail you and the doubts that would assail them.

"It had been our intention that, following this, Virginia would accompany us to Capella Four. But we have been thinking and we believe it would be better if she were to stay here with you."

Martin looked at Virginia and her face mirrored the surprise in his. In a moment she was in his arms and he kissed her. Then they turned to Myza, who had spoken again.

"By your behavior, Virginia, you have proved to be something less than a Capellan. It seems you have always been something less than one of us. For some reason you exhibit some of the primitive traits of the Earth people. Perhaps that is why no male Capellan has interested you. Because you have found an Earth-man who you believe is just a trifle superior to Earth-men, you think you have found someone compatible."

Myza paused, then said gravely, "Since you feel this way, the Triumvirate has decided that you shall become an Earth-woman. That way, when we withdraw our support, you both will go down the primitive path Martin Enders has spoken of so eloquently."

"I—I am to be punished." Virginia looked at him uncertainly. "Is that it?"

"As a Capellan, you have violated rules no other has. Should there be an exception for you? As I have said, we thought all along we must take you with us and we have worked to that end. Now of course you will surrender your Capellan identity by remaining . . . That is, if you still wish to stay with him."

"I still have a choice?"

"Yes."

She looked at Martin.

"I will stay," she said slowly.

Myza shrugged. "As you wish. We have given you every opportunity, but we could not take you along to remind us what we had done without having let you make that decision yourself."

"One moment," Martin said.

"Yes?"

"You are going to leave and take this thing you call a thought reinforcer with you?"

"Of course."

"Don't you think you owe the human race something?"

Myza considered that. "No. I can't say that we do. It may interest you to know my wife and I were born on Electra Three, a planet of Seventeen Tauri. When our colony left that planet, the people there were much further advanced than you are. They were sent back to the primitive ways they had known several hundred thousand years before our kind went there. We have no way of telling, and of course we don't care, what happened to them since. Perhaps the form we made dominant there had succumbed to some other species. If so, it is unfortunate, but of course it can't be helped. The same thing will no doubt occur here."

"How does it feel to play God?" Martin asked. "How does it feel to go in and take a helpless animal and impregnate it with intelligence and watch it grow and then suck its intelligence like a leech to get this thought force of yours?"

"Don't get emotional, Mr. Enders," Myza said quietly. "We realize all that will happen. If there were some reason to perpetuate your race, we'd do it, of course. But you're asking that a civilization such as yours be granted a special dispensation so that it can destroy itself with its new inventions, so that the people can leap at each other's throats without our firm hand to see that they don't annihilate themselves. What useful purpose would the continual warfare your people are famous for serve?" he asked.

"As I told Mr. Klell," Martin said, "all of us are not like that. I, for one, don't want that. I don't want bloodshed."

"What *do* you want, Mr. Enders?"

"I want a better civilization, a people devoted to peace and learning and intelligence and—brotherly love. On our world that expression has become hackneyed. It has, in some cases, become an expression of derision. But that is because it appears there will never come a time when it will be an actuality. People think it is a mark of weakness to admit that that is what they really want, so they ridicule it. Oh, I'm not denying we have primitive tendencies, but there are many of us trying to improve our world. Why don't you give us a chance?"

"I'm sorry," Myza said. "There is no time. None of us would choose to remain here to see this worked out."

"You have helped us this far, why not help us the rest of the way?" Martin argued. "We have reached physical perfection because of the great intermixture of genes. We have got all we can out of physical heredity. Now, with your grant of intelligence, we can assimilate the knowledge that has been man's history. We can start to grow in a new direction—toward each other."

Myza laughed. "You people have barely begun to realize what you can achieve by perception and reason. You should learn that your present chaotic condition is not caused by your lack of ability, but by the lack of reason and your atavistic susceptibility to emotions. The power of your brains is limitless. But what have you used them for? Annihilation."

Martin shook his head. "You are classifying us all under one heading."

"Yours is a lost cause, Martin Enders. I admire you for the plea for your people, but it cannot be done."

"Why?" Martin stubbornly insisted.

"Why? Simply because none of us wants to remain on your backward planet."

"Virginia wants to stay."

"One person cannot run a world as big and complicated as yours. Besides, Virginia would go mad as the only immortal on Earth. She would hunger for someone of her own kind. No," Myza shook his head, "it would never work."

"It could be made to work," Martin said.

"Indeed? Suppose you tell me how."

"*I* could help her."

"You?" Myza was amused. "By the time you died there would be so little accomplished! And she'd have to carry on alone. Besides, what could you, as a mere Earth-man, do to help a Capellan?"

"I need not remain an Earth-man."

Myza looked at Martin sharply.

Martin continued quickly, "You were talking about making me a Capellan, transforming me so I could go along. Nobody seemed to think the transformation was impossible, though you said you couldn't take me along. Why can't you transform me so that I could help Virginia?"

Myza smiled.

"You surprise me, Mr. Enders," he said gravely. "For an Earth-man, you *do* have an uncanny way with your mind, for there is no answer to your question."

"Why isn't there? For the first time in man's history it is possible for him, now that he has achieved so much technologically, to spend more time charting his course through history—*deciding his own future evolution.* It would be possible if you made it so."

"But if he were to progress," Myza protested, "it might be to a more warlike nature, if that is possible. He might eventually be a menace to other existing civilizations on other worlds."

"Not if Virginia and I were here to guide them," Martin said earnestly. "You owe it to the human race you helped raise from a cave-like existence. Now you can make it possible for us to undo the damage you felt you had to cause through your colonization. Why can't the goal be peace and decent human relations? Why can't we work for what is good for man?

"If we could do this, we would be bringing to man, for the first time, a true meaning to life, a reason for effort and being. We would show that man does have a part to play in evolution and that he is capable of great dignity. The mere shadow of morality we have now is a natural product of evolution. Let us work toward a civilization founded on justice and liberty, law and order and on a sound morality. When you came to this planet, it was the dawn of our civilization. Virginia and I want to dedicate ourselves to a brighter dawn—the coming age of man."

Myza studied them. His eyes were cold with thought. His lips were compressed to a thin line.

"It is a noble concept," he said at last. "A plan worthy of Capellans." He smiled. "You love your people, don't you, Martin Enders?"

"I do," Martin said. "I have seen sickness and suffering and war and poverty. I have seen the danger of untruths, of half-truths. If it were possible to change the world, to spread the doctrine of freedom everywhere so that man might achieve his rightful place as the species of the Order Primates as the most selective form of the combination of matter and energy that he knows of, then that would be a good thing and I think Virginia and I ought to be given a chance to do it."

Myza sighed. "Here I had you come, to tell you that you both would return to the primitive state. Now you have offered a plan that would side-step this racial death and make it possible for Capellans to salve their own collective conscience by permitting your civilization to become what it would naturally become through ordinary evolution in millions of years."

The Capellan pursed his lips. "It is odd. An idea from an Earth-man and I find little fault in it. There is one thing, though, and that is, what is to prevent you from becoming virtual dictator of your planet?"

"Nothing, I suppose. But from what I understand of Capellans, what reason would there be if I possessed Capellan attributes? Is it not true that you people control your environment to a considerable extent? What more could I ask? What could Earth people give me that I did not have already, or that I could not create, granted I had your potentialities?"

"You do not appear to be a man with latent criminal tendencies, Mr. Enders. Perhaps you and Virginia could be successful in your operation of a—well, it would be a beneficent dictatorship, wouldn't it? Yours would be a benign influence in the world. You would not reveal yourselves, of course."

"No," Martin said. "To be successful, it must appear the people are responsible for the changes themselves."

"Good."

"There is only one thing that bothers me."

Myza's eyebrows went up a little. "What is that?"

"If I were to be changed—transformed—I would not like to think the thought force responsible came from persons slaughtered in my behalf. Is there no other way?"

"Since we have been ready to depart the Earth, there have been no recent births. There is enough thought force from natural deaths at liberty to now provide the necessary foundation for your transformation."

# 19

A cold autumn breeze stirred up the fallen leaves in the small park, caught them in little tornadoes of whirling debris that moved chaotically, gathering force and then disintegrating against a wall, in a tree, a bush, the papers, leaves and tiny branches falling haphazardly back to the ground.

It was midnight and there was no one in the park. The yellow glow from a few street lights revealed nothing but vacant benches. Occasionally someone, hurrying home from night work, walked across the park, cutting the distance from one place to another. These people were not interested in the grass, the trees or even the moon that rode high in a cloud-blown sky; they came not in pairs, but singly, coat collars turned up, early-morning papers and hands occupying the same pockets, heads down, busy with thoughts.

But wait. There was an anachronism: that couple on the bench, both without coats. They hadn't been there a moment before.

"I still think we should have materialized there," Virginia said. "Coming here only delays what we have to do."

"I still can't get used to this," Martin said. "How do we know he's asleep?"

"We can wait for him if he isn't. Or we can put him to sleep."

"It's cold."

"It needn't be. Make a protective coat."

Martin smiled at her and did. Then he looked away and focused his eyes on a grassy area on the other side of the sidewalk.

"What this time?" she asked.

"Wait and see."

"I know already."

There was a gleam of light that became an electric light about eight feet from the ground.

"That's too garish," she said.

"I'll shield it."

A shade appeared over the light.

"No support?"

"I can't do everything at once."

A steel pole, exactly like others in the park, appeared and

the light, a duplicate now of the others, hung from a cross bar at the top. Below, there was activity. There was metal, gears, a handle, glass, a stand.

"I don't know how these things work," he said.

"You're doing wonderfully."

Finally, the slot machine stood beside the walk, illuminated by the sidewalk light he had created. Suddenly the handle came down, the wheels whirred and in the window appeared three bars. Instantly the jackpot was released and nickels fell from the machine to the sidewalk, jingling cheerfully, some of them rolling up to their feet.

"Having fun?"

"I've got to be sure," he said. "You have the edge on me. You've been doing this all your life."

"You've created a sirloin steak, an automobile, a red head —don't you ever do that again!—a bottle of Scotch twenty years old and now, in a park in Washington, D. C., a slot machine that hit the jackpot at your command. Doesn't that make you sure enough? Aren't you through playing? We have work to do."

"You're just too used to it to get a kick out of it any more. It's new to me."

"All right, you two," the voice behind them said. "Is this your idea of a joke, bringing that thing to the park in the dead of night? You come along with me to the call box."

The gruff policeman they saw standing there meant business.

"I suppose you're going to tell me you can explain," he said. "Well, you can explain it to the judge. Come along, now."

Martin looked at Virginia in alarm. When he saw the look in her eye, he understood. The policeman vanished. So did the slot machine.

"Don't forget the light pole. That would be a dandy for somebody to try to figure out."

The pole and light vanished.

"I didn't know what to call him anyway," Virginia said.

"You really had me fooled for a moment," Martin said with relief. "I thought we had run into our first bit of trouble. I nearly dematerialized all over the place."

He moved closer to her, took her head in his hands and kissed her soundly.

"You don't need any practice this way," Virginia said between kisses.

He drew away and looked at her intently. "I've just thought about something. What about children?"

"You mean—our children?"

"Yes. We'd want them to be Capellans, wouldn't we?"

"They left the thought reinforcer," she said. "We can pick up the surplus thought force any time we want—if we have any children."

"Of course we'll have children." He sat back on the bench. "Now that I know what it's like, I'd want them to be just like us. I feel so whole—so wonderful because the new dimension gives me so much more room than the old. How do people stand it being just human beings?"

"Now you understand how we felt about Earth people," she said. "The thing is, the congenitally blind don't miss sight. They can't imagine what it must be like. So it is with the difference between a human and a Capellan. Isn't that right?"

Martin nodded. "We'll do a lot of things, Virginia. There's so much to be done."

She put a hand on his arm. "But we'll never do it sitting here."

"It's this first one that gets me," Martin said. "I can see the effects of my telekinesis. But this influencing human behavior—that's something I need to practice on."

"Major General Deems is a good starter."

"I suppose we do have to undo the trouble we caused there. Do you suppose he's still looking for us?"

"I fancy so."

"I hope he doesn't feel us materialize."

"You were the only person I ever met who could feel a chill when a Capellan started using his thought force. That's where you differed from others on Earth. That's what made you a difficult subject to control. You broke out of it easily before Dr. Merrill, you remember."

"How can I ever forget it?" He rose. "Well, I guess you're right. No time like the present."

They vanished.

Major General Deems was sleeping very soundly in the upstairs bedroom of his large home a mile from his office in downtown Washington. His wife was similarly occupied in an adjoining room. The door connecting was closed.

An electric clock on the dresser indicated 12:30. A branch of the tree just outside the window occasionally scratched the pane as it was blown about by the gusty wind. Pale moonlight that made a pattern on the thick rug helped illuminate the room.

If the general was aware of the sudden presence of Martin and Virginia, he gave no sign. He slept on.

"I feel like Dracula," Martin whispered.

"You're not after blood, darling," Virginia answered. "You just do as I said. Project yourself. You'll have him eating out of your hand. If you get in trouble, I'll help. But I don't think you'll need it."

Martin went over to the bed, leaned on the foot of it and stared hard at the man lying there.

*"Were you surprised when we vanished, General?" he asked.*

*Major General Deems woke and stared back at him. "Yes. Where did you two go?" He sat up.*

*"We just got tired of the game. What did you do when we disappeared?"*

*"Put the whole CIC on your trail."*

*"That wasn't very nice, General."*

*"No, I suppose it wasn't."*

Martin's heart gave a jump. He remembered similar conversations wherein he was the subject. He had once been as compliant as the general.

*"I want you to remember something, General."*

*"I'll remember it," the general said, friendly and wanting to please. "What is it?"*

*"Virginia Enders and I did nothing wrong."*

*"No," the general said. "Of course you didn't."*

*"You are a busy man. A very busy man, General Deems. You shouldn't be wasting your valuable time worrying about us. If we were caught you'd have to appear against us and that would take time from your other, more important duties, wouldn't it?"*

*"Yes, it would," the general agreed.*

*"Therefore you will tell the whole CIC to stop looking for us, won't you?"*

*"Of course I will."*

*"And then you'll forget you ever knew us or ever heard our names before. It will be as if we never existed."*

*"As if you never existed. I'll remember."*

*"It is very important. You don't want to cause trouble, do you?"*

*"No."*

*"Good. Now what are you going to do?"*

*"Tell the CIC to stop looking for you and forget I ever knew you two."*

*"Right. And now, General, you will go back to sleep."*

The general fell back on his pillow and was asleep instantly. Unconsciously, he drew the covers over where they had fallen from his shoulders and then he did not move.

"How was that, Virginia?"

"Fine," she said. "Almost as good as you were when you

were convincing Myza we should make over the world. You were terrific then, darling. Now don't start telling me I've already mentioned it. I'm going to talk about it until the end of time."

"Virginia," he said, coming over to her. "Did I ever tell you how ethereal your eyes are?"

"Yes, but tell me again."

He did. When he had finished, he looked back at the sleeping general and chuckled.

"That was easy," he said. "But I have big plans now."

"Are they what I think they are?"

"You told me I understood all languages. Is that right?"

"That's right."

"Well, then," he said, going to the window and looking out at the moon riding high in the cloud-strewn sky. "I imagine we're going to take a long trip this time."

"Well, what are we waiting for?"

"I can see the headlines in a few days."

He chuckled. She grabbed his arm.

They vanished.

Fantasy—per se?
Futuristic and/or
future reality!
Food for contemplative
thought...?